THE INVISIBLE MAN OF PIZZA COUNTY

A NOVEL BY

STEPHEN TANNENBAUM

Red Engine Press
Pittsburgh, Pennsylvania

LIBRARY OF CONGRESS CONTROL NUMBER: 2021940929

ISBN: 978-1-943267811 TRADE PAPERBACK

PRINTED IN THE UNITED STATES.

RED ENGINE PRESS
PITTSBURGH, PENNSYLVANIA

THE AUTHOR WISHES TO:

First, acknowledge his wife Shirley's talent as an editor, and her infinite patience in dealing with the text of 'The Invisible Man';

Second, express his thanks to Riv Swartz for her skill as first reader and grammar guru;

And always grateful for the good fortune to have studied fiction writing with him for almost twenty years, the author wishes to dedicate this book to his mentor, Monty Culver.

Also by Stephen Tannenbaum

Novels

Cloris Hughes

Complications

THE INVISIBLE MAN
OF PIZZA COUNTY

A NOVEL

Chapter 1

It was the lunch hour in the office of Sanford Klein, Attorney-at-Law.

The woman had quickly hiked up her skirt, bunched it around her waist and discarded her panty hose on the floor near the couch. Now she grunted in time to her thrusting pelvis, "Uh. Oh yes…uh. Oh dear, yes…uh."

But her urgency was of no consequence to Sanford Klein. He ignored it for an urgency of his own—he was dying.

His heart had hesitated a moment ago, and followed the hesitation with a breathless stumble and a coquettish flutter that reminded Sanford of his wife Millie's eyelashes. He recognized the approach of death; he expected it momentarily.

The woman's legs were crushing him with their greedy insistence. He wondered if death would come first, or if she would—he was scared shitless, but he almost giggled at that. Almost.

It was like Sanford Klein to be frightened to death yet suffer in silence. He was that stubborn. She, on the other hand, was an insensitive woman. She would mistake his cry for an orgasm if he were to cry out, and he refused to give her that satisfaction. So he was silent. To hell with her, he thought. I'll just lie here on her—in her—and die. That ought to put new color in her erotic dreams.

Then he realized that she would think she had fucked him to death. The idea that he had died getting it off would console her. She would thrill to her woman power. It would stoke her pride, damn her. Damn him, too, helpless as he was to prevent it.

So he was to be used again. The idea, once thought, seemed hardly worth a shrug to Sanford—he nearly giggled again. He breathed deeply against the hysteria and clung to the woman's damp, galloping shoulders as if he were riding a wild mare.

What complaint did he really have against her or any of the others? He was in this position—oh, was that a pun?—of his own volition. Millie had warned him that a man with his weaknesses had no business exposing himself—God, another pun—to such a woman.

Millie had said, "They'll suck you dry, Sandy. They'll kill you one day. You know that, don't you?" Her voice quavered as she scolded him. Still, he remembered her lashes fluttering coquettishly despite her anger and fear. "Are you listening to me, Sandy? One day they'll take more than you can afford to give." She snapped her fingers under his small, nondescript nose. "And that'll be it."

Sanford's colleagues would have used legal jargon: a quote of the applicable statute, followed by several court rulings to add the weight of precedent. Millie's warning, while lacking a professional touch, was more incisive: "Bare-assed on a Naugahyde couch is no way to practice law."

Sanford could not pretend to harbor any serious regrets. Still, out of academic curiosity, he wondered if Fate had decreed this end for him, or if he had simply missed a turning, sped unaware past a secondary road that might have altered the course of his life. Perhaps he should have followed the corporate road. That would have been so clean and dry. He imagined that a man could keep his pants on all day long practicing corporate law. In Sanford's imagination, however, lawyers in corporate law sneered down in elegant silence from their fortieth-floor boardrooms at insignificant men such as himself. Sanford would have balked at the idea of inviting himself, his boring, colorless self to a three-martini lunch. The fortieth floor was no place for Pizza County's Invisible Man.

Oh, there again. The second hesitation and flutter were more prolonged, a more breathtaking warning.

"Umph. No…uh, don't stop. Please don't."

Won't, he thought, grunting now at each of her thrusts. Uh…won't stop. Uh…hang on to the very end. Why not…uh?

Why not criminal law? His dear friend, his only friend, Doc Goldenson, was a TV courtroom-melodrama junkie. Doc was hooked on the black-and-white *Perry Mason* re-runs shown late at night on Pizza County's cable network. Doc had watched them so often he could actually recite the dialogue along with the star, actor Raymond Burr. Sanford had spent many an evening watching TV with Doc. While his friend's and Burr's lips moved in sync and the TV reflected blue-white fascination on Doc's face, Sanford had tried to imagine himself in that courtroom, pacing back and forth before a witness, his voice resonating like the actor's with accusation and disdain. The client's very life in balance on Sanford's every word. How ludicrous—Sanford couldn't help sniggering. Even dear, naïve Doc would not have suggested Sanford for such a role.

If neither corporate nor criminal law, what kind of practice was the best fit for Sanford Klein? What clients were the best fit for him? He never actually answered the question or identified the category of client best suited to him. He never found them, but they found him.

His clients were the community's most vulnerable women, the female halves of estranged couples going through messy divorces. Maligned females, stripped of their dignity, femininity and self-esteem by abusive, philandering, conniving husbands: they sought Sanford Klein, they cherished and opened themselves to the very qualities of Sanford Klein that led everyone else to nickname him The Invisible Man.

They didn't mind his drab, rumpled clothes—to them, he was merely being modest and unassuming. Nor did his women clients mind his gray, insipid features—they were docile, calming influences. Nor was his tedious, stolid, hesitant and un-aggressive personality a shortcoming—even his banality, in their eyes, was an asset. They had already been browbeaten and bullied by one member of the domineering male sex. They could not be expected to turn to another bully of the same sex for counsel and comfort.

Yes, there were a few female attorneys in Pizza County, but to tell their troubles to another female would have made the bedraggled wives feel even more miserable than before, would have made every complaint sound like an admission of sexual inadequacy. Sanford Klein's clients preferred a counselor with a submissive personality and an apparently neuter gender, with the sagacity of a Supreme Court Justice, the protectiveness of a big brother and the rectitude of a priest. In their minds, Sanford Klein.

There were few real challenges to the legal side of his work. Nothing more was needed than a basic understanding of the law and the instincts of a hungry dog with a new marrow bone. More than legal counsel, Sanford's clients needed an emotional leg up. They needed to be prodded to stand on their own feet, to rediscover their dignity and self-reliance. Once this was done, they could recognize their own worth and desirability. The challenge for Sanford was finding a way to accomplish all this, a way other than on the

Naugahyde. At this he failed. Before they could reach out to anyone else, his demeaned, emotionally gutted clients reached out to the Invisible Man. Though God knows he tried, Sanford just could not turn away.

There—a third, probably the final warning. Sanford held on, resting his cheek against the damp flesh of the woman's breast, feeling her heaving breath on his neck and shoulder. He wondered if Millie would forgive him for...

"Oh...oh now!" the woman demanded. "Now now now!"

...For going this way, allowing this to happen yet again. Will she, again...uh...again...uh...again?

Both lawyer and client cried out, and Sanford Klein died.

Chapter 2

Miss Helga Shumacher approached her impending retirement as she approached everything else in life—with military rigidity in her slight body and a critical pursing of the lips. The venerable legal secretary had outlived all of her former bosses and cared little for Sanford Klein, her present one. A shriveling thirty-five years of legal paperwork had left the old woman—not an exuberant person at the start of her career—with only two remaining passions: the first, for her daily luncheons at Suterberg's *Vienna Tearoom*; the second, for military precision and strict adherence to routine, which she inherited from her great-grandfather, who had ridden across Central Europe in the cavalry of Otto von Bismarck.

Ordinarily her lunch of unsweetened tea and watercress on whole wheat bread, without crusts, would have been completed at precisely 12:45 p.m., and a crisp march back to her desk would have begun.

Ordinarily, on the way her critical lips would have been pursed and her head, capped by a Teutonic helmet of gray hair, would have wagged at some evidence she had witnessed of the slow but certain decline of Western civilization, such as the *Tearoom's* recent switch from linen to paper napkins.

This noon, however, she left the *Tearoom* ten minutes earlier than usual, in a purse-lipped, head-wagging retreat prompted by the demeanor of a new waitress. The waitress was a large-boned, buxom youth who chewed gum noisily as she moved from table to table and who was obviously wearing no bra under her uniform. The vacuous smile on her farm girl face as she offered to refill Helga's cup could not atone for the impertinent way her flesh flounced—why, it was absolutely bovine. The scandalized Teutonic head was still wagging in Sanford Klein's outer office as Miss Shumacher bent to secure her pocketbook in its place in the bottom right desk drawer.

Bang!

The glass of the outer door was nearly blown out of its frame as Leo Drylie barged in. His basso voice bawled, "Where are ya, Klein, ya rotten sonabitch? Wait'll I get my hands on ya."

Drylie was as short as Napoleon and just as belligerent. He used his booming voice—the only big thing about him, folks said—as an aggressive weapon; he bludgeoned people with his basso profundo. Strangers, startled by a voice of such magnificent depth, would look around for its source and not believe it had come from such a strutting little man.

"I'll wring yer scrawny neck," he bawled.

Most people who knew Drylie, while calling him Little Napoleon behind his back, preferred to yield to his overbearing manner and blustering barrages. Not Helga Shumacher.

"I'll kick yer ass…oop!" Leo's mouth slammed shut when he saw the purse-lipped, flinty-faced woman. She looked as unyielding as the photo of the monocled old Junker, her great-grandfather, that was on her desk.

Drylie said, "Jeez, Shu…er, Miss Shumacher, you startled me. I didn't expect…no." Leo gulped between words as he tried to catch his breath.

Leo Drylie was stockier than Helga, but no taller; when he confronted her directly, her Prussian ice-colored eyes peered levelly into his—to Drylie it was like trying to outstare an eagle.

Unable to gulp enough air to inflate himself properly, he shrank red-faced and breathless from her.

Miss Shumacher feared no man. She considered all the husbands of her boss's clients—especially Leo Drylie—as contemptible little boys. In her view, a sharp reprimand was often called for, and if they persisted with their tantrums, "Well," as she put it, "sometimes a swat on the wrist is called for." She kept handy a two-inch thick, metal-edged ruler for such occasions.

"You have business with Klein, Mis-s-ster Dry-lie?" She asked.

He said, "Damn…er, darn it, Miss Shumacher, I got to see Klein, I got to." His voice shriveled to a pathetic whine, sounding like a diesel with a dead battery. "Something's got to be done about this." He took from his pocket the kind of single-window envelope that always contained an invoice. "Klein must've known The Bitch was gonna send me this."

Drylie had not used his ex-wife Amelia's name in six years. Instead he bitingly referred to her as The Bitch. Miss Shumacher tolerated this one profanity from Leo because she agreed with him—Amelia Drylie was indeed a bitch.

Helga was about to disavow any knowledge of the envelope or its contents when she spotted a determined look in Drylie's weasely eyes. She was familiar with that look, knew the action it preceded: the impudent little swine was going to bolt for the entrance to her boss's private office. She was too fast for him. Before he could do more than lean in that direction, she moved at cavalry speed to place herself between the little man and his goal.

"You'll sit, Leo," Helga ordered. "I'll look at what you have there," she ordered, nodding toward the envelope. "But you'll sit. Now!"

He hurried to the hardwood chair opposite Shumacher's desk, ridding himself of the envelope as if it were hot. After a warning nod to him, Shumacher perused the envelope's contents. Her left eyebrow went up. Leo took that as a sign of sympathy.

He said, "Fair's fair, right, Shumacher? I've held up my end of the bargain. The child support and alimony checks go out right on time, every darn month. I pay everything right on time, just like me and Klein agreed. No man on earth is more reasonable…er, all right." He prevented her interrupting with a deprecating hand. "I made some noise about it, but when my daughter's teeth needed straightening, I came through with the bucks. And not one word of complaint." Another hesitation. "Well, I made some noise, but I paid, didn't I? Every cent?

"But this is too much. The Bitch…she…she." Leo reddened and gulped, finding the words un-swallowable. "A nose job now? The Bitch wants Trudy to have a nose job and expects me to pay? She only lets me see Trudy twice a goddamn month, I can't even remember what she looks like, does she even have a nose, how do I know? Chrissake."

Helga let him rant for a time. When she tired of his carrying on, she tapped the envelope with a bony finger. "Calm yourself, Leo. This is not our doing. I will see that Klein gets it when he returns from lunch."

"Don't gimme that," he interrupted, boldly pointing at the private door. "He's in there. He never goes to lunch, nobody ever seen him eat lunch. He's in there, all right." Drylie was wound too tightly to stop. "Wouldn't be surprised if The Bitch is in there, too. He's prob'ly boffing …"

WHAP!

Miss Shumacher punctuated Drylie's sentence by stamping her foot on the tile floor.

"Must I wash out your mouth with soap, Leo? One more word..." The spinster glanced at her watch. "It's 1:05. Klein should be in now by his private entrance. I'll see." She glared at Leo and commanded, "Stay, Leo!"

He nodded.

Helga tapped lightly on Sanford Klein's door, tried the knob and finding it locked, she used her key.

From where he stood Drylie could see only the half-open door and Shumacher's hand with skin like blue-veined porcelain on the knob. A breath caught noisily in her throat. She was rooted with her hand frozen to the knob, taking rapid shallow breaths and whining like a wounded dog. Drylie ventured to the door, pushed it further open and stood on tiptoes to see over her shoulder.

Klein's partially naked corpse had rolled off the couch onto the carpeted floor. The corpse was wearing a long-sleeved white shirt, faded gray sox and tie, and scuffed black shoes. His flaccid penis listed vaguely left toward a rumpled gray suit coat, trousers and underpants piled on the floor near the couch.

Sanford Klein was, even in death, a dull heap.

CHAPTER 3

As a rule all dentists hate Mondays, but for Doc Goldenson this Monday was proving to be a particular nightmare. It had begun at 7:30 a.m. with a special performance in front of the bathroom mirror. Along with his morning stubble, the ordinarily steady-handed Doc shaved off a chin pimple. The resulting blood gusher should have been enough of a scarlet warning to send him flying back to bed.

Instead Doc proceeded to the kitchen with toilet paper wadded against his wounded chin, to discover that his wife, Celia, had fed the last of the milk to the cat—Doc hated dry bran flakes and black coffee. He didn't much care for the cat, either.

Still, he hadn't realized that it was The Monday of All Mondays until he arrived at his office on Maple Avenue in downtown Sutersberg to find that all of Pizza County was in the midst of a dental crisis. Both phones were frantic, as was Patsy Policastro, receptionist and dental assistant. While Doc hurried past her desk to get into his blue smock, Patsy juggled the phones and the appointment book, her eyes looking harried and her Neopolitan complexion look-ing smudged. And damn! She had neglected to make the coffee.

By noon they had dealt with five toothaches, a lacerated tongue and two acute periodontal pockets, and there were still three toothaches in the waiting room. Doc, feeling like the proverbial one-armed paperhanger, grudgingly skipped his usual lunch with his crowd of friends at *Salerno's Italian Villa.*

Now, at 2:30 p.m. Mike Armbrust was in the dental chair with a five-inch square of latex dam clamped to his lower left molar. Doc was struggling to maneuver a narrow barbed file along the length of the mesio-lin-gual root. Patsy, usually decisive, stood hesitant in the operatory doorway.

Lately Doc was sure it wasn't his imagination, Patsy seemed to be shrinking. She lived with her husband Salvatore, an unemployed coal miner, and Patsy's mother in her mother's house on the east side of Sutersberg. The old lady cooked and kept the house, Salvatore drank and Patsy worked for Doc. Afterward she went home to great heaps of her mother's spa-ghetti, ravioli, gnocchi, tomato pies and homemade bread. Even as a young girl she had been almost as wide as she was high. Now the weight of all that Italian food was compressing the nearly fifty-year-old Patsy; she seemed to be on the losing side of a war against gravity. Doc also noticed that when it got hectic at the office—Mondays, especially—Patsy's hair, straight and black as telephone wire, developed frizzy ends. And when her energy sagged, she began to drop words from her sentences.

"Chief's at door," she blurted. "Wants you, says now."

Armbrust grunted from behind the latex dam—the barbed file had finally slipped to its full length in his stubborn canal. Doc sighed with satisfaction.

"Which chief do you mean?" he asked.

When she failed to reply, Doc glanced up and found her looking more frazzled than usual. There was a warning tightness in her jaw and she looked as if she might stamp a foot in rage—her usual when she was ticked off.

She said, "Chrissake, many chiefs we got this damn town?"

Damn, to Patsy, was a swear word and she rarely swore; Doc knew he ought to back off. But the look of her standing in the doorway in a white polyester uniform, looking to him like a lump of pizza dough, goaded him to tease her further. After all, he was tired, too. He set aside the mirror and file.

"There are two fire chiefs," he said, counting on his latex-gloved left hand, "and the hospital has a Chief of Medicine and a Chief of Surgery. That's four."

Armbrust leaned forward in the chair and added from behind the latex dam, "Railrobe's a gleef angineel."

"Can't understand you, Mike," Doc said, forcing his patient back in the chair. "Forget it."

"Yuns real funny," Patsy growled. "Nuzzi. Know damn well I mean Nuzzi."

Doc found that needling Patsy was no fun. Not only was she too frazzled, but trying to be clever was too exhausting. He took up his instruments and resumed filing those narrow canals of Armbrust's molar. Without looking up he said, "I can't stop in the middle of this, you know that, Patsy. Nuzzi's tooth-ache will just have to wait out there with the others."

"But..." Patsy hesitated, then shrugged and de-parted, mumbling to herself.

When one of the root canals was finally filed to his satisfaction, Doc brightened. If things continued to go well he might be able to get home for dinner at the usual time. But Mike's molar had at least three canals—Doc suspected an anomalous fourth canal in the distal root. So two or three still to go. Even before Doc's optimism had begun to slip away, he heard sounds of squeaking leather and a squawking walkie-talkie coming up the hall, getting louder as they neared the operatory. Then in the doorway stood Dominic Ianuzzi, Chief of Sutersberg Police, all three hundred pounds of him.

"Ya mistake me, Doc," he yelled over the squawk-ing of the walkie-talkie. "It ain't a toothache this time."

"Out out out!" Doc shouted. "For Godsakes, Nuzzi, this is a dental office, not a traffic jam."

Doc noticed that Nuzzi's thick eyebrows were knit into a single dark line across his forehead, underlining the peak of his uniform cap. That eyebrow line, along with Nuzzi's very round brown eyes gave him a perpetually perplexed look. At the moment he was wearing an Official Business face, that of a confused but determined bulldog.

Doc set aside his instruments and asked, "Could you at least shut off that infernal noise?"

Chief Ianuzzi stared from the walkie-talkie to Doc and shrugged. "Sure, Doc, if it bothers ya."

Doc was reminded how difficult it was to do dental work in that little bow mouth as the fat man began speaking into the black plastic case.

"Uh…central, this is Star One repeat Star One, c'mon back." A crackling acknowledgment was followed by, "Uh…this here is Star One at Doc Goldenson's. Got to cover my ears fer a spell. Ring Ma Bell if ya need me." He listened again. "Uh…yup, that's a ten-four and I'm gone." Looking pleased with himself, Nuzzi punched a red button on the side of the case.

In the following silence the sucking of the saliva ejector in Armbrust's mouth seemed especially loud; it drew Nuzzi's attention.

"Who in hell…" He wondered aloud at the face behind the latex mask. "Hey, that you behind there, Mike? I'm damned! Looks like Doc's got yer ass in a sling, if ya get my drift."

"Goddab flumby," replied Armbrust.

Doc stifled his patient, then turned to Nuzzi. "You'd better tell me what the big emergency is, then I want you out of here or your ass will be in a sling. You get my drift?"

"Easy does it, Doc." Nuzzi's belly, cascading over his belt, wobbled when he moved. His belt was cinched deeply into that belly, but the weight of revolver, handcuffs, extra cartridges and taser stun gun made it difficult to keep his pants up. Nuzzi was constantly hitching up black leather and blue serge. That was usually good for a laugh, but when Nuzzi said, "Easy does it, Doc," and hitched up his weaponry, it added menace to the moment.

"What's so damned urgent?" The conviction was gone from Doc's bark. "Can't it wait till I finish with Mike?"

Nuzzi's thick brow line sank nearly into his eyes. "You're kinda upset, Doc. Considerin' what's happened, I ain't surprised. Sure hate to upset ya further, but there's questions got to be answered. Churchy la femme, if ya get my drift? Need to know where I can get a holda..." Nuzzi's conscience nagged at him. "Uh, maybe...maybe we'd best get outa here to someplace private. Ole Mike'll keep for a while."

Doc sighed. The whole town seemed intent on putting some distance between him and Mike Armbrust's molar. He said, "Hear that, Mike? The Law here says you'll keep for a while. I suppose he's right, huh?"

Armbrust's forehead wrinkled and panic showed in his eyes. "Dahellgadub," he grunted, shaking his head.

Nuzzi shrugged. "Suit yerself, but don't say I didn't act considerate. I'd a preferred to speak to ya in private, but…" He shrugged again. "My visit, of course, concerns Klein."

He was expecting a reaction, but got none. "Ya hear me, Doc? Yer friend? Attorney Klein?" Nuzzi leaned over to search Doc's face and nodded eagerly several times.

Doc said, "Sandy? What about him?"

"Wugglebowem?" asked Armbrust.

Nuzzi, ignoring the masked patient, said to Doc, "Don't tell me ya ain't heard? It's all over town. The news leaked outa the Courthouse, reached *Salerno's* before the lunch crowd left. You really ain't heard? Damn! It's all over town."

"For godsake, Nuzzi, what's all over town? I've been so damn busy, I haven't had lunch, haven't been out since first thing this morning."

Nuzzi drew his fat lips into a tighter bow. "Guess that explains it. Well, jeez, it pains me to be the bearer of bad tidings."

Curiosity had drawn Patsy up the hall to stand behind Nuzzi in the crowded operatory doorway. She stared at the back of Nuzzi's head through the lower lenses of her bifocals.

"G' to't already, Nuz." She stamped her foot.

Nuzzi hitched up his pistol belt and trousers and began to recite as if from an official report:

"Sanford Klein, Attorney at Law, was found on the floor of his office in the First National Bank Building at precisely five minutes before the hour of one p.m."

Startled by the rapt attention of his audience, Nuzzi's official demeanor slipped. He threw a fat fist emphatically forward and back, an umpire's out call.

"He's out!" Nuzzi bawled. "Dead as a fuggin' doornail."

CHAPTER 4

Doc felt pummeled, winded and weak in the knees, as if the police chief had worked him over with a truncheon. Leaning heavily on Patsy, Doc retreated to his private office at the rear of the suite and eased himself into the swivel chair behind his desk.

Patsy mumbled, "Mike, tooth, temporary, um, definitely." She hustled out to rescue the abandoned patient.

Doc leaned back in the chair with his eyes closed, trying to get control of his emotions with deep breaths. Nuzzi, with a prolonged audible sigh, lowered his bulk into the chair across the desk from Doc.

Doc opened his eyes expecting to see on the policeman's face…what? Contrition for the brutal way he'd broken the news of Sandy's death? He doubted Nuzzi was capable of contrition. No, he had expected to see a grin on that fat face.

Instead he found Nuzzi gaping at the lithographs mounted on the wall above Doc's head. His little bow mouth was open, his shoulders were down and his arms hung at his sides.

Doc asked, "You seem taken with the pictures, Nuzzi. You like them, huh?"

Nuzzi appeared to be lost in them. He blinked several times to regain focus. He said, "Uh…yeah, I like them. Specially that one of the elephant."

Doc grimaced from a foul taste that had leaked into his mouth from… somewhere. He said, "That one's called, *Elephant Charging through Tall Grass*. Celia bought it for me years ago as a gift to celebrate our opening the office. She says it's still her favorite, says it captures my personality."

He nodded toward another lithograph, this one on the wall to his right—a field of un-mown hay in pencil strokes of beige.

"This is my favorite, Nuzzi. If anything really captures my personality, that one does." Among the tall stalks of hay, a small boy lay on his back day-dreaming at the sky, a strand of hay dangling from the corner of his mouth. "It used to be Sandy's. He gave it to me."

The memory of his friend gifting him with the lithograph made Doc's voice thicken with emotion; he reached for a Kleenex from the box on his desk.

He said, "Sandy took it right off his office wall and handed it to me."

Nuzzi sat up in his chair and paid close attention as if he were about to hear a sordid confession. The look on his face was a classic—a hound that happened upon the scent of a feral animal. He said, "Yeah? Klein gave it to ya?"

Doc blew his nose into the tissue. He said, "He found it at a flea market on the West Coast. He was on vacation, carried it all the way back on the plane from San Francisco thinking it would look nice on his office wall. A lot of trouble for a picture, but he really liked it. And he was right, it was perfect, a breath of fresh air in that dull place of his."

Nuzzi nodded. He said, "Lawyers got the boringest offices."

"When I saw that picture on his wall, I couldn't take my eyes off it." Doc declared, "It's me, Nuzzi."

The policeman leaned forward to stare at the boy in the picture.

"Not *me*, you ninny! I meant, me, the spirit of me. Sandy looked at the picture for a long time after I told him that it was me. He got that grin on his face. You know how he can grin sometimes? No, I guess you don't. His face, well…"

Doc hesitated, not meaning to insult his friend, as if he were listening. "I've decided, after giving it a lot of thought, the right word for Sandy's face is, unremarkable. Everyone in town calls him The Invisible Man, you know. He isn't invisible at all, just very very unremarkable. But he can break out in the biggest grin sometimes, like a Cheshire cat without teeth. My mother used to call that kind of grin a monkey shine."

Nuzzi brightened. "She meant a shit-eatin' grin, didn't she, Doc?"

Doc gritted his teeth and went on, determined not to let Nuzzi's ignorance spoil the memory.

"As I was saying. Sandy broke out in one of his Cheshire Cat grins and said, 'I don't know how I missed it, Doc,' he said to me, 'but you're right. The boy in the drawing is definitely you.' Then he lifted it off the wall and gave it to me. 'It's yours,' he said, and wouldn't take no for an answer."

Nuzzi frowned and shook his jowls. "Interestin' character stuff, that," he said, "but callin' Klein un-remarkable don't jibe with what the D.A. told me. Fact, it sounds like you and the D.A. are talkin' about two different guys." It was apparent Nuzzi held the D.A. in high esteem.

Doc smirked. He said, "John Grimes may be the County District Attorney, elected fair and square, but under the skin he's nothing but a goddamn farmer, Nuzzi. That's all he is and all he'll ever be."

Nuzzi shrugged. "Farmer or no, he's a pretty sharp cookie, Doc. Got his thumb on everything's goin' on in the County."

Doc agreed with Nuzzi on that point: Grimes's grapevine was extensive. Through it Grimes was undoubtedly apprized of everything that happened and everything that was rumored to have happened in Pizza County. And everything he learned Grimes managed to turn to his political advantage. Be that as it may, Doc was convinced that no one, not even a wily coyote like John Grimes, knew more about Sanford Klein than he himself did. Still, he'd better ask.

"What did Grimes tell you about Sandy?"

Nuzzi grinned, giggled as he searched the tiny office unnecessarily for eavesdroppers. "He called, and you'll love this, Doc, seein' as how you feel about him bein' a farmer. He called Attorney Klein the busiest rooster in the barnyard."

It took a moment for Doc—no farming in his background—to get a grip on that metaphor. "What!" He leaned forward in his chair. "Grimes called Sandy, my friend Sanford Klein, a rooster?"

"Yup, he did. And also the cock of the walk."

"That's bullshit, Nuzzi," Doc insisted, pounding the desk. "Pure unadulterated bullshit."

The fat man tugged an earlobe. "I don't think so. Like I said, the D.A.'s got his thumb on the whole County. When he says somethin,' I believe it. When he says Klein was raidin' the chicken coop, you can bet yer ass Klein was raidin' it. Hell, man, the way he died proves the puddin.' You oughta seen it like I did."

The bad taste in Doc's mouth had deteriorated to acid reflux.

"On the office floor, he was, bare ass and pecker. No idea who was in there with him. She musta run off scared when he dropped over."

"No," Doc whimpered, "aw, Sandy, no."

"Plain as the nose on yer face, Doc," Nuzzi declared. If he was aware of the effect of his words on Doc, it didn't show. "Yer friend was humpin' like a steam engine when his heart up an' quit. Sanford Klein screwed hisself to death!"

CHAPTER 5

Doc had been thoroughly bludgeoned by Nuzzi's blunt instrument of a mouth. His own mouth tasted coppery and corrosive from reflux that was now eating away at his esophagus. His friend Sandy had gotten himself into some sort of mess, and only the D.A. could clear it up. Doc's legs felt unreliable, but he just had to move.

Before the fat cop could swivel in his seat, Doc hurried past him.

Nuzzi shouted, "Hey! Hold yer horses." He puffed along the hall after Doc. "I'm supposed to ask about yer Missus."

Through the upper half of her bifocals, Patsy watched her boss pass the reception desk grumbling under his breath. Ignoring a toothache and a lost filling seated in the waiting room, Doc dashed out of the suite onto Maple Avenue.

Being out of doors seemed to ease the heartburn somewhat.

Doc mumbled to himself, "Nuzzi's not bright enough to keep his pants up, he must be mistaken. D.A.'s mistaken, too."

He took one cross street to Main, then wandered uphill in the general direction of the Courthouse. "Damn farmer, Grimes. Doesn't have me under his thumb. Got Sandy confused with...who the hell knows who."

At that moment the Reverend Isaiah Bartlett was performing what he called his *janitorials*, sweeping the front stoop of the rectory of the First Lutheran Church, which he did religiously every Monday afternoon—penance for Sunday morning's sin of long windedness.

"Afternoon, Doc," Reverend Bartlett called to the dentist. "A little late for your noon walk, isn't it?"

Doc continued mumbling to himself, "Nuzzi, the goddamn fool."

"Ah, a waiting room full." The Reverend shook his head regretfully. "There are so many afflicted souls." He returned to his sweeping. Doc hurried on.

Marie Galvanzione, as usual on a weekday afternoon, was seated at her desk by a window that fronted on Main Street. She was the C.F.O. of the *Sutersberg Consumer Discount Company*. Known to the local men as Magnificent Marie, the mini-skirted beauty would sit at her open-well desk facing the sidewalk, often with her legs crossed. One or two oglers always loitered outside the *Consumer Discount Company*. Doc stopped there for a breath before moving on.

The sun was well up, as many of Suterberg's older citizens were fond of saying, and by mid-morning it was raising a sweat on the brows of people as they hustled along Main Street. There was very little pedestrian traffic way up on top of North Main once the early mass had concluded at Saint Anthony's Cathedral. The faithful, many hanging onto caregivers or being pushed in wheelchairs, had already departed.

Further down the hill, though, it was a different story. Down there Main Street was frantic with automobile and truck traffic, orchestrated with honking horns, squealing and chuffing hydraulic brakes.

Doc Goldenson was Piazza County born and bred. He came into the world in Piazza County Hospital, he was educated in Piazza County public schools, and until he left home to attend college and Dental School in Pittsburgh, he rarely ventured beyond Piazza County's borders. It was rumored, and it may have been true, that Doc was one of the young wags who stuck the sobriquet "Pizza" onto the County.

Even though the air was tainted by diesel fumes, a lung's-full of it seemed to refresh Doc. He spotted his barber, Joe Sabucchio, and Saul Stern half a block ahead on the sidewalk in front of *Stern's Swimming Pools & Unpainted Furniture*. Saul bore the nickname Snotty Saul because he had been a mean and argumentative child. The two men, from their wagging heads and gesticulating arms, were raging over the economy or U.S. foreign policy, or the like. Doc purposely risked his life to avoid them by jaywalking to the other side of the street.

The old *Rexall Drug* had fallen victim to the wrecking ball eleven years before, leaving its empty lot as a gap in the block of storefronts that Doc found more galling than a missing front tooth. But there the gap remained despite Doc's complaints between the *Pretty Posy Shoppe* and *Parnelli & Slade, Haberdashers*.

Directly across the street from the gap was *Gunderman's Department Store*. The Chamber of Commerce had provided a bench on the sidewalk in front of *Gunderman's*, again over Doc's objection, for pedestrians to take a load off their feet and to sun themselves on a nice day. Placing the bench in front of *Gunderman's*, Doc had argued, would focus attention on the gap directly across the street. Sitting there would be downright demoralizing, especially for the elderly. They couldn't help making comparisons between the town's deterioration and their own. As usual the Chamber of Commerce chose to ignore Doc.

Doc usually avoided the bench and the people who regularly occupied it, but now he headed for it and them.

"Hi, doc," Bill Smeltzer, a blind man, greeted him. From his perch on a vinyl pad beside the bench, Bill peddled pencils out of a battered brown fedora. Melvina Toth sat at her accustomed place on the bench, and Ernie Norton stood behind it.

"Any of you folks see John Grimes this afternoon?"

Bill made a point of joking that he hadn't seen Grimes or anyone else for that matter. Melvina, instead of answering Doc's question, shoved a sausage-sized finger into her open mouth and touched a tender spot on her gum. She wasn't wearing her lower denture. Doc groaned. He said, "Another sore spot, Mel? That's the third this month?"

Melvina shrugged and withdrew her finger. Doc held up a hand, he was in no mood for a discussion of her recurring denture sores.

"Hhhsss."

Doc turned to the sound, something akin to a balloon leaking air. Ernie Norton.

"Hhhsss—no sign of Grimes—hhhsss—but sit a spell. You look done in, Doc."

Ernie Norton was a retired coal miner and black lung sufferer. Since he could hardly breathe in a sitting position, every day he stood behind the bench, hovering and wheezing. "Fair day fer breathin' though, Doc, I'll tell the world—hhhsss."

Doc couldn't help shuddering. "Jeez…uh, glad to hear it, Ern. You're sure the D.A. hasn't been by here? He usually does, this time of day."

The town of Sutersberg, a prim and promising place in his parents' time, had slipped into a worn-but-quaint period during Doc's young manhood. Now it was unavoidably clear, especially when seated on the bench, that it had slipped further—skidded, really—

from quaint to dilapidated. Doc saw a resemblance between Sutersberg and wheezy old Ernie Norton: it had the same potholes and cracks in its streets that Ernie had in his face; it had the same need for a good scrubbing, some fresh air and replacements for its missing teeth, such as the one left by the old *Rexall Drug*. And as if the town needed further humiliation, the terra cotta tiles of the dome over the Courthouse rotunda, once a gleaming gold color, had been chemically degraded by air pollution and diesel fumes to the color of hotdog mustard. It was a tragicomic kick in the ass to a weary has-been of a town. Doc grieved for it.

He said, "Hang in there, Ern."

One after another, three 18-wheelers trundled past the bench.

Doc rubbed his eyes and shouted over the hydraulic hissing, chuffing and roaring, "I said, hang in there, Ern. You, too, Bill, Mel."

He wondered how Ernie managed to breathe, polluted as the air was by exhaust fumes and the smell of mozzarella cheese from the luncheonette in *Gunderman's* basement. Doc's gastric acids were still refluxing. Though still shaky, he continued to search for D.A. Grimes.

WE SELL PIZZA signs and that odor of burning cheese were everywhere, even though the lunch hour was long past. No sooner was Doc out of range of *Gunderman's* than he reached *Piazza Palermo*, which, like *Salerno's*, served pizza and all the other Italian favorites. Farther along Main were two other parlors that served nothing but pizza; and several nearby taverns had signs in their windows boasting that pizza was available within. Because it did not sell pizza or smell of it, Doc slowed down as he passed the *Mc-Donald's*, but he speeded up again when he reached the *Suds 'n Snack Shack*, which definitely did sell and smell of pizza as well as domestic draft beer. He also rushed past the *MyTeeGood Diner*, that specialized in pizza topped with mashed potato-filled perogies. He also knew that pizza was the *haute cuisine* at each of the Fraternal Orders of Elks, Lions, Moose, Odd Fellows and Optimists; pizza was available, too, at the Knights of Columbus, the Italian-American Club, the Polish White Eagles, the Teamsters Local #30 and the Firemen's Benevolent Association. Nearly every building in the downtown housed a luncheonette, grill or snack shop, and every one of them sold pizza. There was even a WE SELL PIZZA sign in the lobby of the Courthouse—President Judge Kaplovich of Common Pleas Court had a quirky sense of humor. Economic conditions of the 1980's might have shut down the coal mines and extinguished the County's foundries and mill furnaces, but it seemed to Doc that the pizza ovens were belching more fiery than ever. A pall of baking, bubbling, burning mozzarella cheese hung over the entire County.

A man sat at the snack counter of *Bushyaeger's Five 'n Dime*. Doc stopped in his tracks and stared in at him. The man sat with his back to the street; he seemed to be lost in thought as his fingers drummed against the root beer barrel. He was the right size to be Sandy. How many times had Sandy sat on that very stool, tapping out a rhythm on the side of the root beer barrel—was it him? If so, he must have been in an unusually up-beat mood this morning—Sandy rarely felt bold enough to wear navy blue. But the pants were baggy enough to be Sandy's pants, and the coat hung like a rumpled cloak, as Sandy's usually did on his hunched figure. Could it be Sandy? Nuzzi was anything but bright, God knew. Was he mistaken about the dead man's identity? Doc hoped so.

Doc let go of present time, allowed his mind to drift back to Saturday afternoons in his childhood:

Root beer in tall frosty mugs, five cents. Hot dogs sizzling on Old Lady Bushyaeger's grill, his mouth watering at the smell. No memory of the taste, just the smell. Every Saturday the same fun routine: the double feature at the Bijou, *then dash from the* Bijou *to the* Five 'n Dime *to visit the legions of lead soldiers painted blue and red and green; visit the hot dogs sizzling on that grill—what a smell!*

"Only a nickel left from your allowance, eh Goldenson? Too bad." Old Lady Bushyaeger needn't have asked. She would reach into the icebox beneath the counter for a mug, responding with a shrug to his weekly financial plight, "Five Cents, Goldenson. Enough for root beer."

By the time Sanford Klein and his wife had arrived from Pittsburgh, the *Bijou* was one of Sutersberg's missing teeth, and toy soldiers, then made of green plastic instead of lead, were no longer the playthings of grown men. Old Lady Bushyaeger was long dead and the root beer cost half a buck.

Doc had introduced Sanford to *Bushyaeger's* root beer and kept bringing him back for more until Sanford was as addicted to it as Doc was. Then, whenever either man felt low because of a disagreement with a client, a tiff with the wife, a porcelain crown that refused to fit its tooth properly, the call would go out: "Hey, can you get away? Meet me at the barrel." An hour with a root beer and a friend—feel much better.

Doc hurried into the *Five 'n Dime* to greet Sandy. He came out a moment later, downhearted. Other men beside Sandy have baggy suits, average builds and dust-colored hair.

Chapter 6

For the life of him Doc could not recall which friend it was who telephoned the Goldenson home that particular midweek evening.

The caller, whoever it had been, said, "C'mon over for a drink, you and the Missus. The party's already underway." Along with the caller's voice Doc could hear noisy talk and clinking glasses. "It's a come-as-you-are." After a long day, neither Goldenson was eager to go. "Why not? Everybody's here. Even the Invisible Man...least, I think he's here. What, you haven't? Well, now's your chance."

To Pizza Countians, who had known each other for decades and were used to seeing each other almost every day, it seemed entirely logical to want a person's name to fit him or her like a second skin. When the name itself didn't quite fit, a nickname was tacked on; that usually did the trick. There could be found in Sutersberg or in its rural surroundings a Tubby, a Stringbean, a Baldy, a Knuckles, a Diz, a Shorty, a Blinky, a Barrels. It had a Judge, a Chief (or maybe a half dozen Chiefs), a Doc; even a Snotty Saul and a Magnificent Marie. Logic and familiarity, not insensitivity, were responsible, Doc argued. But *The Invisible Man*? It was curious, too, that a newcomer had acquired a nickname so quickly.

After introductions and a few minutes of conversation with the Kleins, Doc wondered if his fellow Sutersbergers hadn't lost their marble. For once he and Celia were in agreement, the Kleins seemed to be a really nice couple. Not noisy or brash or self-centered; they didn't make Doc feel uneasy, as did most big city dwellers.

Though he had lived in Pittsburgh throughout his undergraduate and dental school years, Doc had never gotten over his discomfort with big city people. When he tried to describe the feeling to Celia, she pressed a hand against her bosom—what there was of it—and widened her eyes as if to put him in clearer focus. She would say something like, "You know, I feel the same way when my slip is showing. Maybe you should have that looked into."

That was Celia. Still, Doc had to admit to suffering a bad case of small towner's paranoia: that is, big city men gave him an itch at the nape of his neck that felt as if he were being followed; and big city women turned his neckties into nooses.

But not the Kleins, they and the Goldensons were comfortable with each other. They stood together in one corner of their host's—whoever it had been—their host's dining room, sipping white wine and gathering little pieces of each other's lives: born here or there, went to school where? How long in practice, how long married, how many kids? A daughter? How old? And you? Oh, that's a shame, but no kidding? You look so much younger.

It became obvious to Doc, though neither Klein admitted it in so many words: they hadn't just left the big city, they had fled. They were no more cut out for survival in those dangerous waters than Doc was. There was nothing of the shark in Sanford, no sign of guile or aggression at all. And Mildred…

"Oh…oh no, please call me Millie," she had said, her voice too quiet to be heard over the noise in the room. Her breath was warm on Doc's cheek as she stood on tiptoes to speak into his ear. Millie's eyes—deep, wide, dark brown eyes with long fluttering lashes, reminded Doc of brown-eyed Susans. She whispered, "You must…oh, yes, I insist you call me Millie. I want you both to."

Millie, naïve, vulnerable Millie, would have been constantly frightened by the big city, Doc thought. After a few moments searching the depths of those eyes, he regretted that he hadn't been there to protect her—he would have been strong, courageous, capable of anything. Doc, his six foot, well-fed frame towered over her, the buttons of his shirt straining against his bulk—he sucked in his gut and inflated his chest. He looked around at Celia, hoping she hadn't noticed.

Of course there was no denying his own wife's beauty. Celia Goldenson had the tall, slender, angular body of a fashion model and the pure radiance of skin that seemed to come from deep inside, like that of a fine opal. Her light brown hair seemed an unremarkable light brown color in ordinary daylight, but when it was back-lighted by the sun or by a crystal chandelier, as it had been that moment in their host's dining room, and if she were wearing it cascading to her slight shoulders and over half of her forehead, one would say it shone like honey. And the sensual grace of her movements seemed both casual and practiced at the same time, like the movements of a prowling animal. It was as true of Celia at forty-five as it had been at twenty-five—wherever she went she was followed by hungry eyes.

Yet most people preferred to keep a little distance between themselves and what they saw as a five-foot-eight-inch ice crystal. What should be noted, a dead giveaway to a Pizza Countian: though more magnificent than Magnificent Marie, Celia Goldenson never had been given a nickname. To the casual observer the tough, competent and ambitious Celia seemed to be all angles and edges.

It was a bit of a surprise to see Celia and Millie Klein getting along so well. After a half-hearted attempt to include the men in their conversation, Celia turned her back on them and told Millie about her degree in Drama from Carnegie Tech, and how she had parlayed her training in stage makeup into her present career. She was Tri-County Sales Manager for AnnaMae Cosmetics of New Rochelle.

The two women seemed aware only of each other as Millie, her lashes fluttering and her mouth slightly open, looked up at Celia and nodded. Celia, who ordinarily preferred not to touch or be touched by anyone, took Millie's arm under the elbow and drew her closer.

The two women standing so near each other—the tall, angular, honey-haired Celia and the younger, shorter, darker, rather steamy Millie, with a full honest-to-gosh pair of breasts, talking intimately of 'woman things' as if they were alone in the room—the sight of them had a headier effect on Doc than his third glass of wine.

Millie seemed hypnotized by Celia's talk and the movement of her hands. "To highlight a good feature, but with subtlety, with understatement, hmmm? A shadow here. Here just a light bit of blush." Celia's long fingers lightly brushed the softness of Millie's jaw. "Narrowing, dear. See?"

They reluctantly separated when Millie, noticing the time, said that it was a school night for both their babysitter and for their daughter, Ellie. After the Kleins left the party, the host—whoever he was—asked the Goldensons, "You guys get along okay with the Kleins?" He paused over their affirmative nods. "Say, Doc, maybe you should ask him to join the gang for lunch tomorrow. Yeah, do that. You invite him." Hardly able to suppress his merriment, the host turned away. "Next time you see him."

# # #

That night after a shower, Doc thought how luxurious it felt to wrap himself in an immense royal blue bath sheet, monogrammed with his initials in white, and be able to dry his stomach, chest, back and head all at the same time.

He left the *en suite* bathroom, entering the bedroom swathed in the new sheet. Celia had ordered it especially for him to end his complaints that he couldn't get dry with an ordinary-sized bath towel. He said, "This is really—oh!"

Celia sat at her vanity table gazing vacantly into the mirror. She brushed her hair in long, slow, sensuous strokes. Against her delicate ivory neck and blue satin nightgown, the hair rose and fell, setting off shimmers of honey with every movement.

Doc felt a stunning ache in his groin. "Jeez, Ceilie, You look so beautiful…"

She was jarred by the intrusion of his voice but she stayed lost in thought until Doc propped one foot on the bed and began drying his toes.

He said, "You and Millie Klein really hit it off, didn't you?"

Celia glared into the mirror. Her voice had an edge. She said, "Anything wrong with that?"

"No no," he quickly replied, "I liked her, too, liked both of them. Just never saw you warm to anyone so quickly, that's all."

Celia resumed her brushing. "Millie's a dear. I can't say much about Sanford, but isn't she a dear." She ignored Doc's hesitant nod. "And such an interesting person, too. We talked and talked." Pausing with her head cocked to one side, she wondered aloud, "Or did I do all the talking?" A shrug. She inspected herself in the mirror, turning one way then another. With a grunt, she reached for one of her cosmetic jars.

Doc entered the bathroom and called from there, "Sanford's a nice enough guy, I guess. Mighty quiet for an attorney and rather hard to draw out, but… yes, I liked them both." He inspected his teeth in the mirror and mused at his image. "Wish I knew why they call him The Invisible Man."

Celia said, "I think I'll ask them to dinner this weekend." Then louder in case he hadn't heard. "That all right with you?"

"Hmmm? Oh…fine." He crossed naked to his dresser. Feeling her mirrored eyes on him, he sucked in his belly. "Something wrong?"

"Well…no." Celia bit her lower lip, showing a hesitancy Doc had seldom seen on her face. "I was just wondering. Are you going to ask him to lunch?"

Doc rummaged through his pajama drawer until he found his favorite pair. "I suppose so, sure. I'll prob'ly run into him on the street anyway, so I'll ask him." He hesitated. When their eyes met in the vanity mirror, both of her brows were up and she was blushing.

"Jack? Jack, I can't remember what he looks like. I'm really sorry, I must've spent most of the evening with my back turned on you boys."

He avoided her eyes as he unfolded the pajama bottoms. "You certainly did."

"Well?"

"Hmmm? Do I know what he looks like? Of course. He's about, approximately, average height and not too broad but, uh, not thin either, right? And uh, brown… You remember his having brown hair, Ceilie?" She shook her head. He said, "Or sort of gray? Or…damn! Good lord, Ceilie, I spent two hours with him and I can't remember what he looks like. I won't know him if I run into him. What in hell am I gonna do?"

She shook her head and sighed. "For goodness sake, Jack. Call his office in the morning and invite him by phone."

"But I won't recognize him."

"Oooh god!" She rolled her eyes. "How many strangers will be having lunch at Salerno's tomorrow?"

"Hey, right! The first man walks in the door that I don't know will be Sanford Klein. You're a genius, Ceil. What would I ever do without you?"

She frowned and shook her head, setting cascades of honey hair in motion. She said, "I'm going to brush my teeth. After that…" She said, fluttering her eyelashes at him ala Millie Klein, "If you can work yourself up into a romantic mood?" The left eyebrow rose. "Hmmm?"

# # #

If Sanford Klein had not actually been invisible, if it were possible to see him, why couldn't Doc or Celia describe him? It plagued them for some time. Months later, after a lot of thought, Doc realized that while his brain cells, like everyone else's, could be somewhat dulled by ordinariness, his brain cells were being completely overwhelmed—paralyzed even— by the extraordinariness of Sanford's ordinariness. Dull, nondescript, bland, colorless, insipid—there were no adjectives to adequately describe him. And he seemed to have little personality to speak of. His most noticeable quality was that he attracted no notice. Forgetting him was a brain's way of yawning.

It would take determination and concentration on Doc's part to rivet Sanford in his mind firmly enough to prevent the image of him from vanishing.

Often in the early months of their friendship, he came away from Sanford with a migraine headache. But he kept at it.

Celia was not especially surprised at her husband's stubborn determination, but she doubted that anyone else in Pizza County was capable of such an effort—the average local had too short an attention span, in her opinion.

As for Celia herself, she seemed disinclined to even make an attempt. Instead Doc noticed she had developed the habit of ignoring Sanford as if he were indeed invisible. Whenever the two couples were together, Celia literally pretended Sanford was not there and directed all of her attention and conversation at Millie. When Doc had complained about this, Celia merely shrugged.

Well, indifference was not Doc's way. He was determined to befriend Sanford and…

\#   \#   \#

Right there on the street he declared aloud, "…and anybody doesn't like it can kiss my ass!" Suddenly out of his reverie—so embarrassed—he found himself standing in front of the large window in front of *Salerno's Italian Villa*. Two astonished diners gawked at him, obviously reading his lips.

CHAPTER 7

The sun had reached its three o'clock position in the sky over the west side of Main Street. Doc stood on the sidewalk across from the Courthouse, in its shadow. A light breeze skipped along the street, ducked into doorways and around corners, kicking up dust as it went. Doc tasted the breeze for a hint of rain, as if rain would be an optimistic sign. None. It merely felt rough against his face and gritty on his tongue.

The Pizza County Courthouse was an imposing sight. Its design was meant to intimidate the bumpkins—Doc frowned at it, certain that he was not one of those bumpkins. Greco-Roman architecture had never suited his taste, which ran more to utilitarian than to imposingly ornate. Besides, the Courthouse had always seemed to him to be in acute distress, like a fat lady in a tight corset.

The Courthouse, crowded onto a lot neither deep enough nor wide enough to bear it gracefully, was boxed in on all sides by Sutersberg's four major thoroughfares—Main Street and Pennsylvania Avenue running north and south, Pittsburgh and Otterman Streets running east and west. Consequently, the stone-block portico, the steps up to that portico and the statue of Justice guarding the steps were too near the sidewalk. If that were not enough, the four fluted granite columns that supported the portico roof—Doric, Ionic? Who knew the difference?—looked as if they could use some help. Any time Doc had to enter the Courthouse, he felt as if both the law and the Courthouse portico were about to come down on him.

If you asked Doc, the scales of justice in the hands of a blind amazon was a cornball notion. A lawyer's trick meant to confuse the bumpkins.

As it always did, gawking at the statue and the Courthouse brought to mind his father, Earl Goldenson, who had died in 1971. For no reason that Doc was aware of, his father hated the legal profession and disliked all its practitioners with a passion that was legendary in Pizza County. Earl's outbursts against the legal system struck Doc as paradoxical, since in other respects his father was a reserved man.

Earl Goldenson was a nervous, secretive man, small in stature, pale in complexion, with thin, gray eyebrows that appeared penciled on a troubled forehead. A half-circle of gray hair fringed his head from ear to ear. In a manner most people had thought effeminate, Earl was in the habit of preening his fringe of gray hair with a fine-tooth comb, as if it were a precious pelt. Not surprising, Doc thought, since the man was a furrier by trade.

They hadn't looked alike, father and son, nor had they been much alike in temperament. Doc favored his mother, a robust, light-hearted, sanguine woman. But the two men got along well enough; they spent a fair amount of time together. At least they had spent a lot of time in the same room, though to be honest Doc couldn't recall all that many words passing between them. To his later regret, most of their time had been wasted watching baseball or football games on the boob tube. Had they understood each other or been close? Had they even known each other, really? Doc doubted it.

What they had not watched together on TV were Doc's favorites, re-runs of the *Perry Mason* series. The one and only time they did watch an episode together was the last time, as far as Doc was concerned. In that episode, while Raymond Burr pursued justice for his client, Doc's father spewed invective at the TV set—"Bastards! Bastards!"—as if the very existence of justice, law and order were a conspiracy against him personally. Predictably in that TV episode, as in all the others, D.A. Hamilton Burger bungled the case, which led the old man to shout—"Goddamn, goddamn." He vibrated with rage, bouncing up and down in his chair. "Goddamn incompetent fool, bum lawyer. They're all bums!" Doc vowed never again to watch *Perry Mason* with his father.

Inevitably, one disturbing memory led to another: this one was of the time, at an annual Fall Mental Health Bell-Ringer Ball, when Doc first learned that

Pizza Countians had tagged his father with a nick-name. Doc was standing in the coatroom line behind Leo Drylie. Leo, as usual, was needling his ex-wife. Amelia, ghastly under fluorescent lights, her fading, tanning-parlor tan looking like jaundice. Amelia dressed in a red sleeveless cocktail dress with a mink jacket thrown over her shoulders against the October chill. Drylie, cheap bastard, staring at that jacket, imagining his last several alimony checks sprouting wings. His basso profundo voice whined, "Don't tell me, I can guess. You bought that jacket from Earl the Squirrel." Amelia's spitting anger only encouraged Drylie. "I know dead squirrels when I see 'em."

Earl the Squirrel? Doc preferred not to dwell on the possible connections between the nickname, the fur business, his old man and his old man's hatred of lawyers.

While Doc didn't necessarily agree that ignorance was bliss, there were so many times when ignorance did promise to be more blissful than the truth, it became his habit to slam a mental door in the face of all gossip. Who was playing around, and with whom? Whose marriage was on the rocks? Whose teenage son was caught smoking—smoking what?—in the high school boy's rest room? Why had his father been nicknamed Earl the Squirrel? Doc chose to have no idea.

He and Sanford Klein had been good friends for three years before the news leaked over the transom of that mental door of Doc's that Sandy was the most successful divorce lawyer in the County—no mean feat for Doc, considering that *Salerno's* was across Main Street, cater-cornered from the Courthouse, and that most of the men who lunched with Doc every day were, nominally at least, Sandy's colleagues.

Entering the restaurant each day, Doc would shout, "Order in the court, you shysters!" to his lawyer cronies. They seemed not to mind; they returned his jeers with ones of their own, pointing into gaping mouths at pretend sore teeth and accusing Doc of fumble-fingeredness. But Doc would merely scoff and serve them with writs of mandamus, habeas corpus, amicus cureii and res ipse loquitur. After such boisterous preliminaries, they would settle down to pizza and whatever gossip was being whispered around the Courthouse. Yet Doc failed to hear any of that.

Doc was glad when he learned of his friend's success, but he could not imagine troubled women—any women, for that matter—placing themselves in Sandy's hands. The thought struck Doc as ludicrous. He frowned and sighed. Why did women insist on doing the opposite of what he expected? Not understanding women ran in the Goldenson family, as did grousing at lawyers. Was it possible that women were drawn to Sandy? And when they placed themselves in his hands... Doc shook his head vigorously. He'd been wrong before, but never *that* wrong.

Chapter 8

Doc was about to step off the curb to jaywalk across Main Street when he was grabbed from behind. The man who grabbed him said, "Whoa up there, Doc, y'ole hoss thief."

No mistaking the twang of John Grimes, as usual, trying to hide his education out behind the barn. He did so habitually even in ordinary times, but for him these were not ordinary times: it was an election year in Pizza County and Grimes was fending off some stiff competition. So stiff was the competition that Grimes was sounding less like a local farmer and more like a Tennessee hillbilly.

The tall, wiry D.A. had a thick head of black hair and a rather woeful face. He bore a resemblance to Abraham Lincoln and he milked the resemblance for all he was worth.

Doc thought he looked more like David Carradine and would sometimes throw a fake karate chop at Grimes. Not now, though; Doc was in no mood for such antics.

Grimes said, "You seem a mite agitated, ole fella." With a sage nod, he put his arm around Doc's shoulder.

"I'll give you an old fella," Doc growled, shrugging him off. "I'm agitated, all right, thanks to that fat-assed police chief of yours."

"Talked to Ianuzzi, did ya? Thought maybe he missed you."

"Oh no, that bastard never misses. He barged into my office like a freight train and told me… The things he said about my friend…" Doc made a bow mouth and imitated Nuzzi, "Said, 'Yer friend Attorney Klein humped hisself to death. Klein was found bare-ass and peter on his office floor.'"

The D.A. winced. "Said it that way, did he? 'Humped hisself to death, bare-ass and peter?' I'm truly sorry about that, ole friend, truly. Nuzzi meant no harm, y' know, he never does. He's not too bright, is all."

"Not too bright? Is that what you call him? The man's a sadist, a goddamn sadist." His jaw ached from grinding his teeth. "Don't shake your head at me. Nuzzi's a sadist and an idiot, and you know it. You oughta know it, he's your man. But I don't blame Nuzzi as much as I blame you." Doc tapped Grimes on the chest to direct his anger. "Nuzzi was only repeating things he heard from you."

To prove that point, Doc quoted the police chief as having accused Sanford Klein of rooster-hood and of scratching about the barnyard after divorced hens, words obviously right out of Grimes's mouth. The D.A. nodded sagely.

"And there I was," Doc went on, "mourning my best friend's death when I find out Nuzzi wasn't even talking about Sandy. He couldn't have been. Sandy was no rooster. By no stretch of the imagination was he a rooster. Who'd know that better than me?"

Grimes took Doc's arm and refusing to be shrugged off this time, led Doc toward the crosswalk.

"Where are you taking me, you demented hick?"

"T' my office. How about a little nip of the 'home-made'?"

Doc felt a need to hurt Grimes, but he didn't know how. He wrinkled his face to look like Mr. Yuk and stuck out his tongue at him. The ridiculously juvenile gesture seemed to have worked, the startled Grimes released his arm.

Doc pleaded, "Can't you put away the farm boy act long enough to clear up the confusion?"

For a few silent moments the two men searched each other's faces.

They were born-and-bred Pizza County boys; close enough friends to be the exception to the rule about town kids and farm boys not getting along. They'd been together in a one-room elementary schoolhouse, then in junior high and high school. They had boarded the bus together heading for college in Pittsburgh. John climbed onto that bus still wearing the overalls he'd worn doing the morning's farm chores. The stink of the farm was still on him.

The two men read each other's faces for what seemed an unnaturally long time. The sad truth was there to be read in Grimes's eyes; it was painful to bear but undeniable. Doc felt as if he were sinking into the sidewalk.

He said, "So it's true what Nuzzi said? They found him that way, naked?" Grimes nodded. "The bit about the rooster and the hens, that was true, too? I can't believe it, John, I just can't."

Doc discovered a wad of bubblegum stuck to the pavement, gooey from the heat and peppered with grime. Both men stared at it. Doc probed it with the toe of his shoe and drew out a pink strand of gum, stretched it until it snapped.

Finally Doc said, "Sanford Klein was my best friend. He couldn't have been a rooster without my knowing."

Grimes groaned, "Doc. You must be joshin' your ole buddy. You're the last man to know what's goin' on right under yer nose."

"Since when am I so damn naïve?"

"Since forever. Since the fourth grade. You were the only kid who didn't know about the birds and the bees. Same in high school. Took you the longest time to figure out how Jeannie Lucas earned herself the nickname, Lucky."

"I figured it out."

"You didn't."

"Did, too."

"Didn't, least not till her luck ran out, you didn't."

Embarrassment, noise, traffic fumes, heat and a recurrence of acid reflux, all were working on Doc to make him feel dirty and sick. He said, "Ancient history. So I was a naïve kid. Big deal."

"Naïve kid, naïve man, I always say." Then Grimes seemed regretful and pulled Doc around to face him. He said, "Joshin' aside, Doc, I think you know I wouldn't lie to ya or say anything on purpose to hurt ya. We've been friends too long for any of that. Sanford Klein didn't deserve your friendship and... aw, hey. He wasn't worth yer tears." He offered Doc a handkerchief.

Doc had his own. He used it to wipe his eyes and then he blew his nose into it. "Don't be concerned, John. I'm okay. And I know you're not intentionally saying things to hurt my feelings. You're right, we've been friends too long for that. But I still think you and Nuzzi and the other know-it-alls are wrong about my friend Sandy." A gesture with an open palm. "Maybe I don't know what's going on under my nose, but I do know...knew Sanford Klein. He was a good man, the best. And definitely not a rooster."

Grimes shook his head. "What can I say, Doc? You're just like The Lady here." He extended an open hand toward the Statue of Justice that guarded the Courthouse steps. "Well meaning, but blind as a bat."

CHAPTER 9

Doc pulled his car into traffic only to find himself behind the left half of a double-wide mobile home that was being trundled down South Main on a flatbed trailer. There was a large yellow sign on its aluminum-sided rear end—CAUTION EXTRA WIDE LOAD—as if anyone inching along in that traffic needed to be told. The air conditioner in Doc's car ticked, then wheezed and belched hot air. Doc could kick himself for forgetting to get it fixed.

The somnolent pace of traffic and the hot air had Doc in such a listless state that a close chuff-chuffing of air brakes barely roused him to glance in the rearview mirror. What he saw behind him was the front end of an old Mercedes diesel truck hauling cattle feed, its grill looking like a grinning mouthful of chrome teeth and gums. It was ironic, being stuck between an extra wide load and a farmer—his position between Grimes and Nuzzi—ironic, but he wasn't amused.

What he was amused and pleased by was something the D.A. said before they took leave of each other in front of the Courthouse:

"Go home, Doc," Grimes had said. *"Talk it over with yer Missus. Celia knew Sanford Klein at least as well as you did. Prolly...uh, prolly better."*

As far as Doc was concerned, Grimes's implication that Celia was somehow involved with Sandy was proof positive—Grimes and Nuzzi and all of the County's other know-it-alls were dead wrong. Why, anyone who actually knew Celia, especially anyone who knew her habit of turning her back and disregarding Sandy, would realize that...

BLAAT!

At the edge of town where Main Street expanded into a four-lane limited access highway, the other vehicles shook off their torpor and began whizzing past Doc and past the extra wide load. Doc was unaware of them until with a blare of its horn, a roar and a trailing slipstream of blue smoke, the farmer took off past him. Doc made a right turn into the Oak Hill Plan, in which he and Celia and the Kleins lived, along with many other families of Pizza County's well-to-do.

After coming to a stop at the first intersection, he sat with the engine idling while he tried to decide whether to make another right, which would take him to the Klein house on Green Orchard, or should he turn left to his own place on Peartree? The proper thing, no doubt, would be to go to Millie. She'd have been notified of Sandy's death three hours ago by someone more tactful than Nuzzi, he hoped. But just in case that fat clown had been the one to break the news, Doc vowed to kill him if Nuzzi had said anything hurtful, anything at all. If Millie was told how they found Sandy—bare ass and peter—oh Lord, what a thing to happen, what a calamity!

Startled out of his reverie again, this time by the sound of a circus calliope blaring *How Dry I Am*: BOOP BOOP BOOP BOOP.

A red Corvette snorted at Doc's tail pipe, pawed the asphalt behind him and pulled alongside. Doc took an instant dislike to the teenage boy behind the wheel, who yelled, "Wake up, y' old fart!"

The boy's passenger, an adolescent girl with stringy blond hair and the most vacant stare Doc had ever seen, stared blankly at him. As the Corvette swung past Doc toward Green Orchard, sounding another BOOP BOOP BOOP BOOP, the girl inserted her little finger derisively up her right nostril.

Doc grumbled, "Jeez, we're in for it when that generation takes over." But that settled it. Rather than follow those two, he turned left toward home. Millie needed firmer shoulders to cry on than his were at that moment.

CHAPTER 10

So far today had been a more miserable Monday than usual, and it was probably naïve to expect a change of luck. Still, Doc hoped to find Celia's purple Cadillac in its slot in their garage. In his opinion, the *AnnaMae Cosmetics* saleswomen didn't need Celia as much as he did at the moment. Sometimes a man needed to cry on his wife's shoulder, even if the shoulder was bony.

Although he could recall at least one exception, Celia was usually a rock in a crisis. He expected her to be a rock in this one, even if she were somewhat shaken by Sandy's death. Her involvement with Sandy had been casual. To her he had been an inevitable but ignorable presence, a part of the package in which Millie was wrapped, along with their daughter Ellie and Ellie's Brownie Troop, that Millie den-mothered. In order to have Millie's devotion, Celia had to accept Sandy. So she did, and nothing more.

Celia might possibly suffer remorse for treating Sandy so neglectfully, Doc thought, but she would undoubtedly spend most of her sympathy on Millie. He didn't mean to accuse Celia of callousness, it was just the way of all women, rather than mourn the loss of a man, to mourn the plight of the widow. Although he admitted to being a failure at understanding women, Doc knew with a certainty that it was different with men: his best friend's death ached deep in his bones, like rheumatism, and he knew it would persist. He would always see Sandy drumming impatiently on the root beer barrel at the *Five 'n Dime*. He would always wonder if Sandy had remembered to brush his teeth.

He remembered:

Back to the 1960s. Around the outpatient clinic of the Pitt Dental School rumors buzzed louder than the drills that the Carnegie Tech *Dramats* were loose women. Once that word got around, it had been impossible to keep the dental students away from Carnegie Tech's Fine Arts Building. Either the rumors were wrong, however, or Doc had managed to fall in love with the only *Dramat* who wasn't loose. But fall in love with her he did, like the proverbial ton of bricks, despite what seemed to be Celia Morgan's—she had changed her name from Morganstern to Morgan for professional reasons—her determination to confuse him, occasionally frustrate him and occasionally bruise his male ego. After Celia came to be known as his girl, whenever she managed to say or do the exact opposite thing from what he expected, Doc would feel as if everyone were laughing and staring at him. He would blush mightily each time his Celia ordered coffee in a Chinese restaurant, or paraded into an anti-war rally at the head of an ROTC precision rifle team. Or when, one freezing Thanksgiving day, Celia attended the annual Pitt-Penn State football game dressed like a Hindu in a blue silk sari, with a caste spot on her forehead.

Could those incidents have been premeditated to provoke him? Doc was suspicious Celia was purposefully provoking him, but she swore with hand on heart and wide innocent eyes that she meant no such thing. Doc believed her. Some people just naturally marched to a different drummer, he supposed. But later, when he happened to see a TV special on the life of Isadora Duncan, he began to wonder if Celia hadn't decided to pattern her life after Isadora's. If true, she was portraying that passionate, unpredictable spirit with great aplomb.

From the moment of their first meeting Celia refused to call him Doc. He'd actually been called Doc long before dental school; he'd been called Doc back as far as grade school. He'd been dubbed Doc by Pizza Countians who thought it laughable that a ten-year-old boy would want to be a dentist rather than a cowboy or a fireman or a furrier like his father. Even his mother had accepted the nickname. He'd been called Doc for so long, his real name might've been lost forever, except that to Celia it was Jack this and Jack that.

A lot of white water had run under their marital bridge in the past twenty years, and Doc had only one regret: they were childless. He knew this was no more Celia's fault than his own, but if he were a vindictive man, or a bitter one, childlessness—son-lessness, daughterlessness—might have destroyed their marriage. Instead they had meticulously avoided discussing it, though he had been tempted to bring it up whenever Celia raved about Millie's parenting ability with her daughter Ellie. It made Doc's teeth ache to think of all the energy Celia wasted on selling face powder for *AnnaMae of New Rochelle*. What a wonderful mother she might have been if only…if only.

But if Celia was as troubled by childlessness as he was, she didn't show it. Or at least she had stopped raising the issue with him. He'd heard that a lot of women with willowy figures were horrified by the very idea of pregnancy. But he shook his head. Celia was anything but neurotic. Besides, when he thought about the way her ass swayed when she walked, it did seem ludicrous to imagine Celia pregnant.

He remembered:

It was the second day of Christmas recess, 1961, and the only students still around were on their way off campus carrying luggage. Their breaths could be seen to condense in front of their faces as they hurried across the Arts quadrangle, intent on abandoning the place. With vacancy as palpable on campus as the chill in the air, Doc didn't blame them. The ivy-covered old quad buildings were dusted with snow. The newer buildings, of aluminum and steel, were decorated with sparse lines of colored lights, holly wreaths and paper chains, now wind-torn and neglected. Everything on campus—especially Celia Morgan—looked sullen.

"It's really dreadful here, Jack," she complained. "Desolate as the North Pole." With each word she seemed to shrink further into her loden green car coat. "No use going home, my parents aren't there. Can you believe it? I can't. I never dreamed they could be so damn thoughtless, taking a Caribbean cruise at Christmastime." She filled her cheeks with air, ballooning them grotesquely. "Bloating themselves with spaghetti on some Italian boat and leaving me behind to fend for myself. I'm the lone soul on campus."

Celia displayed a lot of petulant lower lip, reeled weakly, as if about to pass out, and pressed the back of a hand to her forehead.

"I'm gonna die," she declared. "If I have to be alone on campus for two whole weeks, I swear I'll die."

Feeling more than a little bit on the spot, but not really minding all that much, Doc invited Celia to spend the Christmas holiday with him and his parents in Pizza County. Celia had never spent time in a small town, and seemed delighted at the prospect. She clasped her hands under her chin and pirouetted.

She said, "It sounds absolutely marvelous, Jack. Wonnnderful. Oh, to be with some really real people for a change!" Her voice dropped to a conspiratorial level. "And it'll give your parents a chance to meet me. Their first look at the girl you've been talking so much about. Right, Jack?"

He nodded and smiled weakly while inside he frowned uncertainly. He *had* talked to his parents about Celia, hadn't he? Well, he had mentioned her a time or two, for sure. More than a time or two. How serious about Celia was he, after all? Very serious, he answered his own question, serious enough to bring her home to his mother, even though he realized his mother would jump to the obvious conclusion. He knew his mother would start dreaming of a wedding and grandchildren.

Celia's face was brightly lighted with the sweeping wind and with the improved prospects of the upcoming holiday—she was bright as a Christmas ball. She said, "You won't be sorry, Jackie dear." Her voice, at first husky with promise, quickly changed to a school teacher's tone. "But right now you'd better get to a phone and make sure your mother knows I'm coming." Celia whined, "Jaaack? Why the frown? Most mothers don't like surprises. I'll bet yours doesn't, or am I wrong about her?"

The drive to Sutersberg during Christmas recess, 1961:

Celia Morgan never stepped into or climbed into a car, she hurled herself in—it was the only graceless thing she ever did—she hurled herself in as if she were hurling an old book bag. Once in she would take from her purse the longest cigarette on the American market. In those days it was considered avant-garde by the *dramats* to chain smoke extra-extra-long, filter-tipped cigarettes. After rapid, shallow in-suckings, out-puffings and off-hand swipes at the clouds of smoke, Celia would launch bursts of chatter into Doc's right ear: a show biz up-date, items from *Variety* or other trade papers, bits of gossip from the rehearsal rooms of the Fine Arts Building. The news would burst and sputter from her like steam from a boiler with a bad pressure valve. Doc had never enjoyed being in a confined space with anxious company, but he found himself looking forward to automobile rides with Celia. Like intentionally reaching for a live wire, driving with Celia gave Doc a masochistic kick.

As they drove east toward Sutersberg that December afternoon, an extra-extra-long cigarette did make an appearance, but a word burst of news did not. Celia was strangely subdued. Her impatient replies made Doc's attempt at conversation sound like an interrogation. When, in front of the Goldenson home, he opened the passenger door and offered his arm, Celia uncharacteristically took it and leaned heavily on him. Doc was afraid her legs would not support her. He figured she was suffering a bad case of stage fright.

But she recovered quickly. From a deep chest full of air she seemed to draw the courage to take a few tentative steps toward the house, and seemed to gain strength enough to swing into what Doc and his buddies in the dental school called the TW, the

Tech Walk. First the pelvis, for somehow her entire body trailed behind the pelvis, then the lower half of her swung into a certain rhythm, hips swaying from side to side and buttocks bumping it out. Doc wasn't very musical, but he was told it was a samba. All the *dramats* walked that way, causing a great deal of drooling and eye-popping on campus. He had been told they rehearsed the Tech Walk by going from class to class with their books balanced on their heads. He believed it.

Before they were halfway between his car and the house, Celia had let go of his arm and proceeded under her own sexy steam. Doc hung back for a better view. She took hold of the wrought iron railing and sway, sway, swayed up the concrete steps to the porch.

Doc wriggled on the car seat. The memory of his parents waiting and watching his and Celia's approach sent ripples of yearning and regret through him.

The thirty-five-mile drive from Pittsburgh to Sutersberg seemed to have been a trip of twenty years back in time, and Doc was able to see familiar things with a new clarity: there on the porch was his mother, wearing a polyester pantsuit, white blouse and matching flats. Could there be a more familiar figure than a guy's mother? Yet she looked bigger and more blockish than he remembered; suddenly she looked an era behind the times, all of Sutersberg did. Was that his father standing next to her? Earl Goldenson looked small and faded, as if a dry-clean-only version of him had been washed at home, and had shrunk. Earl seemed confused and off-balance, leaning against the porch railing and staring open-mouthed at Doc's girlfriend.

Celia approached Earl without waiting for Doc to catch up. If any words passed between Celia and his father, Doc didn't hear them. He saw Celia offer her hand and he saw his father take her hand, but then Earl seemed not to know what to do with it. He looked desperate, like a hound that had caught the scent of an alien creature.

Then Celia turned to his mother.

Esther Goldenson passed away in 1974, surviving her husband by only three years. Doc missed them both, of course, but he suffered the deep pain of loss, a rheumatic ache in the bone, for his mother. Despite the pain, whenever Doc thought of his mother, a bouquet of chuckles bubbled up in his mouth and his rib muscles twitched as if her memory had poked him there.

Esther was a formidably built woman—tall, bleached blonde, buxom and sturdy. But her physical presence belied an ebullient spirit and a light heart. She raised Doc on praise and trust. She never reprimanded him verbally, she merely allowed him to see a shade of disappointment in her eyes. That look of disappointment was always followed by a tousling of his curly hair and a teasing poke in the ribs. That jolly good woman rode herd on his growing up with such a gentle rein that he was hardly aware of her bit in his tender young mouth.

The opening exchange between Celia and Esther Goldenson, at least the exchange that Doc and his father were able to observe, was a simple "Hello, Mrs. Goldenson" and "Hello, dear, it's nice to meet you," but before they had said anything to each other, Doc thought he saw something happen between them: in a brief space of time, less time than it takes for a bird to flap its wings, it seemed as if Celia and Esther had taken the measure of each other, decided they approved of each other and had forged a lasting peace. Doc wasn't sure that such a thing was possible, so he wasn't sure whether he had seen it or simply imagined it.

Doc watched as his mother, after welcoming Celia to their home, took her lightly around her waist and turned toward the front door. Esther was remarking on how slender Celia was and how she hoped to fix that with some home cooking as she led Celia inside. Before she was beyond the door and out of Doc's sight he saw Esther glance over her shoulder and nod to her husband. Earl was in a hurry to follow the women, but before he did that Earl stood before his son with his arms folded over his chest, silky gray eyebrows creeping toward each other, nodding repeatedly, perhaps re-evaluating him. Then he went in.

Doc sighed in relief.

Chapter 11

Those awkward moments of first meeting aside, the holiday in Sutersberg proved to be a pleasant respite for Doc. Freed for a time from the rigors of his dental studies, he managed to sleep each day until noon, enjoyed his mother's excellent cooking—which she did constantly in an attempt to fatten Celia up—and watched lots of football on TV.

For Celia, relieved to have scored points with Doc's parents at their initial meeting, she was able to relax and enjoy their company and that of all the other Sutersbergers they introduced her to, those *really real* people she had looked forward to meeting.

It was apparent to Doc that his father couldn't get enough of Celia. Throughout the week of her stay Earl fawned on her, and when he wasn't fawning on her—whenever Earl thought no one was looking—he gaped at her. Doc wondered if his father wasn't sizing Celia up for a fur.

For Esther Goldenson the days flew by too quickly for her to notice them, she was that busy in the kitchen working on the promise she'd made to herself to fatten up this elegant wisp of a girl her son brought home. This beautiful maybe daughter-in-law to be. This please God, maybe, mother of her grandchildren. Esther would not succeed in fattening her up, but she gave it her best effort. Doc had never seen Celia consume so much food, before or since. As to the other thing, well…

After that visit of 1961 Doc would catch his mother sneaking accusatory glances at him, as if it were his fault Celia was all skin and bones. To be sure, Celie was nowhere as slender as she had been in her undergraduate Tech *dramat* days. She had put on a pound or two in a few wonderful places. But it had taken twenty years to happen; his parents never lived to see it. Or grandchildren, he mused.

Had his mother always longed for a daughter? It seemed so, and Doc forgave her. But he could not forgive his father's obsession with Celia. Doc had seen a few of his classmates hypnotized by swaying asses, but his father?

Earl had but one topic of conversation—Celia: her grace, her charm, the innocent appeal of her eyes, her willowy figure. In an attempt to break through to the budding dentist in Doc, Earl even brought up Celia's dazzling smile.

"She's got a lovely smile and beautiful teeth," Earl said, watching in vain for his son's grudging admission. "Or doesn't that interest a dental student?"

During the Spring break of the following year, 1962, Celia was away visiting her parents in New

Jersey and Doc was at home in Sutersberg. After Sunday dinner Doc was reading the sports pages when his father entered the room, humming. Earl took a seat in his favorite recliner and made a pretense of leafing through a news magazine.

He edged into conversation with, "I been doing some thinking about skinny women." It was not a topic of conversation Doc thought a guy should have with his father. He slammed down the paper and rose to leave.

"Hey, what's a matter, what's the big hurry? You got a bus to catch?" The old man had a determined set to his jaw. He was intent on getting something said; there was no hope of avoiding it.

With a noisy exhalation, Doc dropped back into his chair.

"Always in a damn hurry. Would an experienced man's opinion hurt? I should say, not. Now. The way I got it figured…" He checked over his shoulder. "By the time a woman is thirty-five, the ones who were… ahem." With his hands he shaped a Coke bottle in the air. "Built, you know? The ones who were built, by the time they're thirty-five they get fat and dumpy. You seen it happen, right?" He drew a huge bosom on himself and sank deeper into his chair. "Boy, do they get dumpy."

He sat up again. "But Celia, at thirty-five Celia will just be starting to put a little meat on her bones. Can you imagine?" Earl was awed by the idea; it seemed to have dried him out. His tongue probed around inside his mouth, searching for saliva. "Can you imagine what she'll be like with a little meat on her bones?"

Shaking his head brought Doc out of his daydream. There was no point in denying, he'd fallen for his father's vision of a meaty Celia. Was he ever a chip off the old blockhead.

"Damn!" He spotted a car parked in his driveway, all right, but even from a distance he could see that it wasn't the purple Cadillac. It was Chief Ianuzzi's black 'n white. What did that fat jerk want?

Chapter 12

Seeing the police cruiser parked in the driveway, Doc expected Nuzzi to be inside the house with Celia, but as he drew nearer the driveway he saw a man wearing a white cowboy hat was slumped behind the wheel. He recognized the hat as belonging to Nuzzi's second in command, Sergeant Poke Perkins. Doc eased his car to a silent stop close to the rear bumper of the black-n-white.

The late afternoon sun seemed lower in the sky than usual, its work almost over for the day. It looked weary enough that it might drop into a neighbor's yard. It was reflecting dully off the bald head of Chief Ianuzzi, who was on the passenger side of the vehicle using the window sill as a pillow. Both Nuzzi and Perkins were fast asleep. Doc imagined the inside of the cruiser sounded like a sawmill.

The temptation was too tantalizing to resist—Doc leaned on the horn. It jolted the two cops into the air as if by 10,000 volts. Poke's hatted head thunked against the roof and Nuzzi's left temple cracked against the upper window frame and his right ear dropped onto the sill.

What a shitty day, Doc groaned. Even a prank as innocent as that one had backfired. Now Nuzzi and Poke, all the more dogged for being dull, would be looking to get even. That thought gave Doc a stomach cramp.

After collecting themselves and straightening their uniforms—it took Poke several minutes just to uncrumple the cowboy hat—the two policemen became still and stared directly forward in the direction of Doc's two-car garage door. There was no need to hurry. If they exchanged any words, they did so without moving or turning toward each other. They knew who the prankster was or they were guessing who it was, and for the moment they were content to imagine beating him to a pulp, savoring each blow as they imagined it. Clenching and unclenching their fists for tighter grips on imaginary truncheons. Doc stayed in his car while the two cops took their goddamn time.

Their movements were deliberate when they finally stepped out of the cruiser. A salacious grin broke out on Nuzzi's face when he saw that it was indeed Doc—as he'd expected—parked behind them. Poke settled and re-settled his hat until it was settled on his head just so, the brim obscuring from view his hard black eyes. He was much younger than Doc, a different generation, they were virtual strangers, and Poke's eyes frightened him. They were not only hard and dark, but too close together in a hawklike, humorless face. A man to be avoided. Doc knew little of Poke except that since he wasn't a patient of his, Poke probably had bad teeth.

Poke was dressed like his TV hero, Marshall Matt Dillon of *Gunsmoke*. A tin star was pinned to the left flap of a leather vest that Poke wore over a summer-weight, blue uniform blouse. The rest of his outfit—cowboy hat, tailored jeans, pointed-toe boots and quick draw holster lashed to his thigh with a raw-hide thong—was in violation of the Sutersberg Police uniform dress code. His boss, Nuzzi, was a rumpled character in his own right and felt no compulsion to reprimand his second in command for that violation.

The two policemen sauntered spaghetti-western style in Doc's direction, each with one hand gripping his pistol belt while the other hung loosely at his side. Doc knew Nuzzi was simply holding up his pants, but he was worried about Poke: violence was as much a part of him as the perpetual scowl on his face. If he got carried away by the situation, who knew what Poke might do? Doc didn't know Poke well enough to predict, but it would surely be something Doc would regret. As he clambered out from behind the wheel, Doc kept his hands in plain sight, and with a few hurried steps met the two cops between their car and his. He thought meeting them halfway would ease the tension. He was wrong.

"Nuzzi, Poke, heh heh. You guys okay?" Doc tried to control his nerves with a deep breath. "Accident, that, heh heh, with the horn, I mean."

"Accident, my ass" Poke said.

"We know all about accidents, Doc," Nuzzi said. The fat man mopped his brow with a red and blue hankie, then with a grunt he bent to use it to polish a scuff on the toe of his right shoe.

Doc said, "I want you to know how much I appreciated your kindness, Nuzzi, coming to my office to break the bad news. I'd never expect a busy guy like you to…" He hesitated, shrugging. "And, well, here you are again come to make sure I got home all right. Damned thoughtful of you, really."

"You're outa yer fuggin' tree," Poke growled.

Nuzzi flapped his wrist at his deputy. "I'll conduct this, uh, little confab, if you don't mind, Officer Perkins." It was Nuzzi's no-nonsense tone. Poke stopped talking and drifted back out of Doc's line of vision.

"It wouldn't be right, Doc, my taking the credit," Nuzzi said. "It was D.A. Grimes's idea, he sent me." He hitched his pants. "Both times."

Doc couldn't bring himself to speak. It was coming, he thought, the getting even was coming. He wished he'd stayed in his car.

"No, I didn't come to yer office to break the news, I thought you already knew it." Nuzzi's eyes glowed. He gripped his belt with both hands and rocked on his heels. "I thought everybody in town knew it by then. No, the D.A. sent me to find out where yer missus was."

Doc cursed to himself. Nuzzi was gloating and Doc felt his control ebbing away. It was obvious what was coming.

"We need to know Celia's whereabouts at approximately, oh, let's say between noon and one o'clock." Nuzzi scratched his head.

Doc could say nothing, do nothing. Was it just inertia or paralysis that enveloped him? What was to come seemed inevitable; he waited for it.

Nuzzi looked about to pop his shirt buttons. He said, "We need to know her whereabouts. Ole Bare Ass and Peter wasn't all by his lonesome when he humped hisself to death. You get my drift? We need to know where yer old lady was."

Now! resounded in Doc's brain. ***Bash that fat smug face now***! The words jarred him out of his inertia, crunched it into tiny friable fragments, like bits of glass. He moved to obey, reared back to bash the fat smug face. And…

Hearing a movement behind him, Doc tried to turn. He wasn't quick enough. Out of the corner of his eye he saw Poke surging forward. In his hand was something hard and black, aimed at the back of Doc's head.

WHUMP!

A concussion sharp and decisive. An elephant stepping on a raw egg, dazzling and final. A sudden pain, and Doc's brain bubbled red and boiled over.

# # #

There is color to pain; that was a revelation to him. He was struggling to climb the inside walls of a whirlpool of pain, the color of which was red as blood. If the spinning would only slow, he wished; if only there were less motion and the color were darker, he'd be able to see and possibly climb out of the raging red pain.

In answer to his wish, the red slid down the color spectrum to brown, then became purple, black and gray, until it settled into the leaden dullness of a moonless night. Suspended somewhere between consciousness and unconsciousness, Doc saw himself in a massive vaulted chamber of sandstone blocks, a forbidding place of arched ceilings and deep gothic shadows. A seemingly endless center aisle divided the vault into two sections, each of which was lined with crowded pews. The occupants of the pews— were they worshippers?—sat as if frozen; they stared straight ahead, their attention riveted on something at the front of the vault. Unable to see it in the gloom, Doc felt compelled to continue forward along the aisle; he did so hesitantly. There was no movement from the occupants on either side, but they made eerie, moaning sounds which Doc found chilling. The interminable walk and their moaning reminded him of a windy night in a graveyard.

Through the dead-cold light he saw an altar at the end of the aisle. As he neared the altar, his approach seemed to affect the mourners—he intuitively perceived them to be mourners—the closer he got to it, the louder they moaned and the harder they strained to be still, as if they feared their movement would provoke the release of something evil.

Doc was deathly afraid of this place and of whatever it was at the end of the aisle. But the more he feared it, the more he was drawn to it. He couldn't stop his plodding progress forward.

Now he was close enough to see it: a crude, rough box of white pine, a simple coffin with wood handles on the sides. With its lid propped open. His moans joined the others. Advancing to view the remains, he felt himself grow cold, knowing even before he was near enough to see the occupant of the coffin, knowing that it was…

Chapter 13

Meee! A siren wail of fear echoed through every cell of Doc's body. He struggled for several moments against the panic before realizing that his death had been part of a nightmare. His head ached, his eyes throbbed and his heart was desperately trying to burst out of his chest. Convinced that even in hell the dead never had to suffer such pain, Doc assumed that he was alive.

He wondered why his fingers were tingling and discovered that his arms were folded across his chest; that was anything but reassuring since he found himself lying in a confined, well-padded place. He tried to convince himself that it wasn't a coffin, wasn't a coffin, and he wasn't dead, wasn't dead.

Judging by information from only his ears and nose—he was afraid of the searing pain that would result from opening his eyes—he gathered he was stretched out on his living room couch. Testing the air, he recognized many odors as the same ones he'd noticed that morning before leaving for the office: mozzarella cheese and pepperoni from the pizza that had been the previous night's dinner, Mitzi the cat, whose litterbox odors had insinuated themselves into all the fabrics in the house, and a trace of the lemon-scented dusting spray that Celia used.

But Doc noticed odors that had not been present earlier: odors that emanated from one person who, from time to time was heard to mutter curses: the strong smells of tobacco and rubbing alcohol. Doc realized it was their family physician, Dr. Samuel Bronstein. And two other people were in the room: he recognized the voices of the sadistic duo, Nuzzi and Poke. They were pleading in muffled tones with a third person who smelled as if he had stepped in cow manure, so John Grimes was there, too. And another person who reeked of chlorine. Doc couldn't identify its source until the person spoke to Dr. Sam in the machine-gun fashion that Doc recognized as belonging to Stuts Sabatine, the man who drove the ambulance for Mutual Aid Emergency Service.

"Uh-uh-uh, how's his p-p-pupils, Du-Doc?" Stuts asked.

Dr. Sam muttered at Stuts, then the odors of alcohol and tobacco wafted nearer to Doc. His one eyelid was rudely pried up, and he found himself staring into Dr. Sam's watery, faded-blue eyeball while Dr. Sam stared back into his. Something clicked. Before he realized what it was and could attempt to defend himself, the beam of the physician's penlight cut into Doc's eyeball.

"Aawww, Saaam!"

Doc's wail startled Dr. Sam into losing his grip on the eyelid.

"Jack?"

Celia had been standing at the far end of the room. Her voice sounded hesitant and strained until she crossed to the couch; nearer, it seemed to regain its usual strength and certainty. "Can you hear me, Jack? Jack?" Her voice became insistent; the throbbing in Doc's head intensified. Still, he was glad she was finally home.

He was grateful for the touch of her hand on his shoulder, but after a moment she became more insistent and her grip tightened. She's gonna shake me, he thought horrified. Since his throat and lips were desiccated and incapable of anything but grunts and cries, he tried telepathy: *Don't shake me, Celia, please don't...*

She shook him.

He groaned in anticipation of pain—there was none. Doc felt fragile as glass, but obviously he wasn't as badly hurt as he had thought. He was about to consider opening his eyes when he smelled 'Daring Blush,' the latest fragrance from *AnnaMae of New Rochelle*. It was a very delicate rose scent. Beneath that scent was another one, the familiar scent of Celia herself. She was kneeling beside him. He felt her lips near his ear, her warm breath tickling the hairs of his sideburn. He smiled.

"Celia?"

Nuzzi made a remark that Doc suspected was lewd, since it elicited a guffaw from Poke, an admonition from Grimes and a string of curses from Dr. Bronstein. Doc forced his eyes open.

The west-facing picture window was draped to shut out the harsh glare of the setting sun. In the dim light, Celia's face looked smooth and radiant, like fine china.

Intruding on his study of her face was an acrid smell that took him a few moments to identify—bug bomb. Bugs Bagley, the exterminator, was peering at Doc over Celia's shoulder, his brow wrinkled with concern. Bugs's round, leathery face had always reminded Doc of a catcher's mitt.

"What the hell are you doing…" Before the question was even half-asked, Doc remembered that it was Bugs's day to spray for ants and spiders. My God, he thought, there is a mob in my living room. He decided to sit up.

Bugs seemed pleased to see Doc making the attempt. A wide grin opened like a pocket in his face. He said, "Hi, Doc. What's up? Mind if I get on with spraying now?" While he spoke Bugs kept a wary eye on Celia. "While you been nappin' my supper's been gettin' cold."

Doc sat up—OOOW!—then regretted it.

"My goddamn head!" He felt as if his head were swelling to the size of a pumpkin, then shrinking to the size of a pea. It swelled, shrank, swelled, shrank and each change was accompanied by a blast of intense pain. His eyes filled with tears. "OOOW!"

The second yell set off a flurry of motion in the room: Dr. Bronstein chased Bugs and Stuts from the house with a string of curses, Nuzzi and Poke skulked out at John Grimes's insistence, Celia hurried to the kitchen at the Doctor's order to fetch an ice bag. Grimes trailed his men as far as the foyer. Dr. Bronstein wrapped an elastic tourniquet around Doc's bicep, swabbed the arm with an alcohol pad and darted a vein.

As he worked Dr. Bronstein grumbled insults at his patient through his graying, tobacco-stained mustache.

"Some people never learn, never grow up, damn 'em." He released the tourniquet and slowly pumped the contents of the syringe into Doc's bloodstream. "Scrapping in the street like a damn fool." He withdrew the syringe and folded Doc's arm over a gauze pad. "Should've known when I delivered you, I had a damn fool on my hands, I should've known. Fighting in the street at your age, damn fool."

Doc inhaled the familiar odors of the old physician and found them comforting: rubbing alcohol and mildewed tobacco, as if Dr. Bronstein had left his cigars out in the rain.

"This one fights with the cops yet. I should've known I had a damn fool on my hands," he grumbled, taking the icebag from Celia and forcing Doc's head back on it.

He turned to Celia and asked, "You think you can manage this big jerk, dear? I gave the damn fool enough Demerol to ease the pain but not enough to knock him out." He examined his patient's pupils as he spoke. "Try to keep him awake till you're sure there's no concussion. I won't leave if you don't think you can manage." He studied Celia's resolute face. "Ummhmm, you can manage."

The Demerol had turned warm and syrupy inside Doc; he felt it first lapping at the barbed edges of his pain, then flowing over it.

Bronstein packed up the medical gear in his tattered satchel and told Celia, "Keep the damn fool off his feet for a while. What he needs is rest, lots of rest."

From his coat pocket he retrieved a gnarled Italian cigar in the shape of a leprechaun's walking stick; he hung it from the corner of his mouth. "Poke is damn clever with that blackjack, give him credit for that. I've seen his victims before, and not one concussion among 'em. But to be safe, look at the damn fool's eyes now and then, and call me right away if they look funny."

He stood on tiptoes to place a dry peck on Celia's cheek, aimed a final expletive at his patient and stalked out of the house.

Waiting in the foyer, John Grimes stared after Dr. Bronstein, wishing he too could leave. With Nuzzi and Poke also departed, he was feeling friendless and without allies. He returned to the living room and gingerly approached the couch. Celia was once again on her knees beside Doc. Grimes peered over her shoulder at him. Celia turned. The skin of her face, usually lustrous as porcelain, looked cold and dull as plaster.

Celia said, "You. Haven't you caused enough trouble for one day?"

Grimes recoiled from her and gestured at Doc. He said, "I'm, you know, sorry about all this, but we've gotta talk, you and me."

Celia's lip went up in a snarl.

"Okay, not now, not now. I'm, well, awfully sorry, you know?" He backed toward the foyer and the front door.

Celia watched him go. She kept a vigilant eye on him, holding her breath until his car coughed to life and backed away. Then she let her breath out, tossed her head to shake the D.A. out of her hair and returned her attention to her husband.

"Jack?" Her voice echoed in the now finally quiet house. "Jack, I know you've had a pretty rough time the last few hours."

Doc nodded. Watching her closely, he caught her stealing a glance at her wrist watch and, to his surprise, biting her lower lip, which he couldn't recall ever having seen her do. He was touched by her anxiety, but he would have preferred something more positive, such as a neck and shoulder massage.

"But you have to realize," she continued, "it's been rough on everybody, not just you. Understand? You're going to have to force yourself... Damn it, Jack, stop whimpering. I'm saying I don't have time to coddle you. Act your age or, damn it, I'll walk out and leave you like this."

Despite his blurred vision, Doc tried to focus on her face. It was remarkable that anxiety hadn't diminished her beauty; if anything, it heightened it. But he couldn't imagine why she was so upset. It was an effort to move, yes—his arms felt like concrete—but he wished he could pat her cheek.

"Gee, Ceilie, take it easy. You know I hate seeing you get all upset. Didn't you hear Dr. Sam? My head's too hard, I'll be okay. So I got conked, big deal."

"Big deal? Oh my God! You don't remember." Her jaw dropped and her eyes widened. She finally squeezed them shut, and when they reopened, they no longer looked startled, merely curious. Her voice was hushed. "You've forgotten about Sanford." She bit her lip again and a tear from the corner of her eye ran along the side of her nose.

Doc groaned. Poke had bludgeoned all of it—Sandy's death, Grimes's accusations, Nuzzi's innuendoes—right out of his head. Now they were back with a vengeance, as if he were reading it all on Celia's face, which was now pale around the mouth, blotchy red at the cheekbones and mascara-smudged under one eye.

"You forgot all about it?"

His voice rasped against a sob. "Aw, Ceilie, what a day it's been. What a shitty day." She frowned and nodded. She was more upset by Sandy's death than he'd expected.

Doc asked her where she'd been all afternoon.

She answered, "The usual places for Monday. New Stanton, Connellsville." She shrugged. "If you wouldn't tune me out every time I talk about work, you'd know my routine. It's the same every week. I've got the County divided into four sections like pizza cuts. Mondays I work the southwest cut. I touch base with all my sales reps, every one between here and Uniontown."

It was hopeless, or Doc was. No sooner had Celia divided the County into pizza cuts than his mind began to wander.

"I can visit the other areas any day I like, but the southwest cut has to be hit every Monday. Those gals, the weekends play hell with those gals." She stuck out her tongue and blew them all a raspberry. "Bffftt. Without a pep talk on Mondays, their sales volumes go right down the tube."

His mouth was desert-dry and his lids were heavy. He kept losing Celia in a swirl of shimmering images: disheartened saleswomen, hawk-like Poke Perkinses, grinning Nuzzis, nodding Grimeses and several Celias who appeared relieved to have changed the subject to business. Or was that his imagination?

"I was finishing up at *Federman's Dry Goods*," Celia was saying, "when old man Federman himself... Jack Goldenson, have you tuned me out again? Damn it, did you hear any of it?"

"Aw, Celie, I can't concentrate." He touched behind his right ear and winced. "It must be the Demerol. One moment my head is throbbing, like right now, and I think the Demerol is wearing off. Then everything starts shimmering like Jello. It's confusing, awfully hard to concentrate." She touched his forehead and cheek. Her hand was cool. "I heard most of what you said, Ceilie, honest I did. You were talking about old man Federman."

"Um hm." She pursed her lips and rolled her eyes. "I was saying, old man Federman himself came to the cosmetics counter and told me I had a phone call. It was one of my reps, Kate Prinkey from South Sutersberg. You know her, don't you? She was lunching when the news about Sanford reached *Salerno's*."

Celia pressed her bosom and grimaced, looking the way Doc had felt earlier when he'd tasted bile. "Did you know, people were giggling, Jack? Kate heard them giggling and making lewd jokes. Some men were actually drinking toasts."

"Ex-husbands of Sandy's clients, probably," Doc said, "the rotten bastards."

Sounding angry enough to bite, Celia said that she'd rushed out of *Federman's* and sped toward Sutersberg on the Interstate. Doc's eyebrows went up. The very day they'd opened the Interstate, Celia had begun a boycott of it. The only advantages of living among the bumpkins, according to her, were the leisurely pace and simplicity of life. She considered the Interstate an interloper, a symbol of encroaching urbanity, so she boycotted it. Her attitude toward the Interstate—toward Pizza County in general—amused Doc, since no one in his opinion had done more to lead the bumpkins astray than Celia. Hadn't she recruited an army of housewives and marched them out of their kitchens? Hadn't she seen to the placing of their toddlers in day care centers? Hadn't she sent them out, clutching sample cases of *AnnaMae* cosmetics, to canvass their territories? Interloper indeed. Still, Doc had admired the doggedness of her boycott. He was surprised that Sandy's death was enough to get her to drive the Interstate.

"Did you tune me out again, damn you?"

He said, "I didn't miss a word. You raced home. But, Ceilie, on the Interstate?"

Her knee cracked when she got up from the floor. "Move over. No more kneeling, my knees can't take it."

Celia had used a public phone to call Doc's office. "It occurred to me as I was driving along that the news might not have reached you. So often you don't seem to…well, anyway, I was still half an hour from home, and it was driving me crazy to imagine poor Millie all by herself at such an awful time."

She massaged his brow with insistent fingers, as if his flesh were *PlayDoh*.

"There are calls to be made, things to be arranged, flowers and things for the, you know, the funeral. I didn't want Millie to have to cope with all that." A chill entered Celia's voice and her fingers began to hurt him. "I wanted you to hold the fort at Millie's till I got there, so I called your office."

He moved his head from under her fingers; she tapped several times on his left ear.

"And Patsy told me you'd run out of the office with that…" She wrinkled her nose. "…that fat cop chasing you. Really, Jack, two grown men running and fighting in the street like silly little boys." She shook her head and frowned. "You men, all of you, choose the strangest times to regress to childhood."

"That is the way it looked, I guess." Doc couldn't argue.

He tried to sit up, but Celia placed her palm on his chest and held him down. He had no will to resist; he blamed the Demerol.

"Call me a silly little boy if you like but, Ceilie, why's everybody being so rotten? I don't understand it."

She massaged the back of his neck with one hand and with the other forced his lids to close over the tears. She said, "What difference does it make now? Whatever the reason, he's just as dead."

"True enough, but you don't laugh about it, do you? Not in his friend's face? I won't stand for it, Ceilie. Call me a little boy if you like, but I won't. Hell no, I won't."

Doc raged, his neck muscles standing out thick as ropes, but the rage ebbed quickly, and he began to whine. "Nuzzi and Poke and that damn farmer, Grimes…"

Celia murmured to him, as if to a colicky child. "Yes, Jack, all right. Shush now, calm down."

"But you don't know what they've been saying. If you only knew." The Demerol began to affect him again, Celia's voice echoing as if from a long way off.

"I doooo, Jack, I know what they're…I dooo."

Doc's eyes popped open. With strands of hair drooping beyond her forehead and makeup smudges on one side of her face, Celia looked as if she were at the end of her rope. In spite of that, it looked to Doc as if his concern amused her.

"I know what they've been saying, Jack. I wish you wouldn't worry about it. There's no reason to, believe me, there isn't."

"You do? You know everything?"

She shrugged. "What I don't know for sure I can guess."

It made no sense for Doc to deny what seemed to be common knowledge about Sandy. "Why didn't you tell me? Why didn't he tell me? He could've told me, we didn't have secrets between us, did we? I didn't from him. Whenever we needed a good listener, a friend, he had me and I had him. We could tell each other anything, at least I thought we could. Wasn't that the way it was?" His eyes met Celia's, pleading with her. "I thought it was that way, all those times at the *Five 'n Dime*, all that root beer."

"Listen, Jack," she insisted, taking his chin, forcing him to meet her eyes. "I think it's time you stopped talking, and stopped speculating. Too much has happened today. You're exhausted, you can hardly keep your eyes open. According to Dr. Sam, you're not allowed to sleep yet, but you need to rest." She was in no mood for objections. "Please, dear, do as I ask, okay? No more talking and no more speculating. If you try to figure things out now, you'll only jump to wrong conclusions. Oh…" the thought stopped her momentarily. "You've already jumped to conclusions, haven't you?"

Before Doc could reply she glared at her wristwatch—she looked dismayed. Opening the drapes, she verified that it was evening. She groaned, "Oh Lord, poor Millie. The whole day's gone and she's all alone over there."

With some difficulty Doc sat up and stared out the window. Dusk had always been his favorite time in summer. He felt he could see the air draped like sheer blue gauze between the grass and the sky. He'd told that to Sandy a few weeks ago, knowing full well that Sandy wouldn't laugh. He didn't. Instead he admitted to Doc that summer dusks affected him, too, that they seemed to pacify him, gave him a more detached perspective on the passage of time and the futility of his longings. Doc remembered him saying something like that: the futility of his longings.

"Well, look who's sitting up," Celia exclaimed. The sight of him off his back galvanized her into action. "Good." She went to the kitchen and returned with a glass of water. "In case you're thirsty. You stay put while I go over…"

"You're not gonna leave me…?"

She talked over him. "While I go over to Millie's, which I should've done hours ago." She cut off his protest by adding, "Which I would've done except for the conduct of a certain bad little boy." She wagged a finger at him. "Really, Jack. She'll think we've deserted her."

CHAPTER 14

Go tell an exhausted, emotionally punished, possibly concussed middle-age man to rest but try to stay awake. *Go ahead*, Doc thought as he awoke, *see what a waste of breath it is*.

It was the odor of burnt coffee tickling his nose that woke him. There was a pillow under his head in place of the ice bag, and he was covered to the chin with a blanket. Obviously Celia had discovered him asleep, had given up on Dr. Sam's orders and had played the good nurse. He had no idea when she had done it, but she had—a comforting thought. The drapes closed out all but a bright, narrow slice of the morning. Last night Doc thought he would never sleep a wink, his mind was churning so rapidly. That was the last thing he remembered. Now he sat up and felt surprisingly well.

He found his glasses and wristwatch on the dust cover of his stereo turntable, obviously placed there so he wouldn't overlook the note taped to the power button. He sadly recalled Sandy's promise to teach him how to wire in a new woofer in the left speaker, which had blown out when the cannons fired at the

end of *The 1812 Overture*. Doc had planned that re-
pair project for the coming weekend. Momentarily
he wished Celia had chosen some other place for her
note; then he shrugged, trying to resign himself to
being perpetually pricked by little barbed reminders
of Sandy.

When he first stood up, he felt like a toddler. He
noticed after putting on his glasses that he'd been
off his feet for nearly twenty hours. Cursing Poke
Perkins, he ripped the note from the turntable. It had
the appearance of a scribbled afterthought, as did all
notes from Celia. The handwriting tumbled downhill from printed salutation to complimentary close,
looking as if her business notepaper had fallen into
the hands of a fourth grader:

FROM THE DESK OF CELIA GOLDENSON

Jack,

Can't wait for you, Millie needs me.

*Come over when—if—you can. Coffee's
ready, help yourself Don't worry about
the office—Patsy cancelled the next
few days.*

CELIA GOLDENSON
COUNTY COORDINATOR
ANNAMAE OF NEW ROCHELLE

Doc frowned at the note. He ought to ask Patsy
to cancel yesterday as well; that way Sandy would
still be alive.

"Shit!"

He lumbered into the kitchen—the burnt coffee smelled like oven cleaner—and yanked the electrical cord from the wall outlet. He poured the dregs down the drain. He toasted a slice of white bread and washed it down with tomato juice. There was a throbbing ache at the back of his neck and right shoulder blade; aside from those he was free of pain except for the bolt of lightning that struck whenever he touched the spot behind his ear. He cursed Poke Perkins over and over as he left the kitchen.

It was a bright, warm afternoon; it felt great to be outdoors. Doc inhaled huge chests full of air that tasted sweet, green and tarry. He felt muddleheaded and clumsy as he walked along Peartree Way; felt as if he were wading through *crème de menthe*. He wondered if he was drunk.

He went around the corner to Green Orchard Lane and up the half block to the Klein house. People had often told Doc that the house suited Sanford Klein to a tee. Now Doc saw what they meant: it had a dreary, depressing look. Doc had accused the real estate agent who sold the house to the Kleins of insulting the nation for having called the place *American Colonial*.

It was originally an ordinary white, clapboard-sided two story with faux shutters and a mansard roof; it wasn't depressing until Sandy insisted on adding his own personal touch to it. Doc had insisted that it didn't need repainting; Sandy disagreed. Sandy hired a painter who managed to custom-blend a color to suit Sandy's taste—flat taupe. As Doc stood on the street staring at it, the house looked dull. It looked even duller now and would probably look duller still a moment after that. Even on a bright day such as the present one it, like Sandy himself, tended toward invisibility.

Where was Celia? There was no sign of the Anna-MaeMobile, no sign of movement in the house and, odder still, the house was shut up tight. This time of year, Sutersbergers were in the habit of leaving their houses open. Doors and windows were for keeping out foul weather, not intruders. Occasionally a teenager would get into a bit of mischief, but professional burglaries were rare. Nuzzi and his Courthouse cronies took all the credit, of course. They gloated over their police force and its ability to maintain law and order. What a laugh! The truth, according to Doc: professional criminals didn't live in Pizza County, they lived thirty-five miles east of Sutersberg in what most Countians called *The Big City*, and they had more work there than they could handle. Too much to bother with Sutersberg.

As he studied the house Doc's mood dipped to his hollow stomach. The house glowered darkly back at him. Could Celia be chauffeuring Millie on some errand? No sooner did the possibility come to mind than he dismissed it. Millie was in there alone, Doc knew it as sure as he knew that Nuzzi, Poke and Grimes had been no kinder to her than they had been to him.

Millie knew the whole dirty truth, and he dreaded facing her alone. Had she, like Celia, known it all along? He shrugged and headed for the front door.

CHAPTER 15

Doc tried the doorknob; it wouldn't turn. It sickened him to have his fears confirmed: poor, beleaguered Millie had barred the door, raised the drawbridge and flooded the moat. She was trying to shut out the hostile world. But where was Celia?

When the nausea had passed he rapped on the door and called, "Millie? Millie, open the door. Celia? Millie?"

No reply.

He went around to the back of the house, climbed three steps to the peeling, redwood deck and approached the sliding patio doors. He pressed his nose to the glass and shielding his eyes from the glare, peered into Sandy's den.

What appeared to him were probably visual tricks of shifting, contrasting light, but to him it appeared to be an enchanted scene:

It was dark in the den, none of the lamps were lighted. All four corners of the room, the bookshelves on the far wall, the couch to the left and Sandy's La-Z-Boy to the right, all were in deep shadow.

The sun, behind Doc at the moment, shone through the glass and cast his shadow onto the den floor. Millie was stretched out in the La-Z-Boy, her legs in the shaft of sunlight, with dust motes dancing at her feet. The La-Z-Boy was in its fully reclining position and Millie's legs were raised. Her skirt was all the way up to—Jeez! To her thighs. Doc saw white underpants with yellow lace trim. And smooth, full, inviting thighs.

He called, "Millie?" His mouth was so dry, his voice sounded pebbly. He longed to touch her thighs and cursed himself for being a rotten bastard. He shook himself and rapped on the glass. "Hey, Mil? Millie?"

She finally moved, carefully. She set a tumbler on the floor as she up-righted the recliner. As soon as her face came out of shadow, Doc noticed her cheeks were flushed. She had been watching him, he thought as his own cheeks began to burn. He groaned, suspecting that she had been awake all along, watching him ogle her crotch. For a moment Millie looked somewhat dazed. She licked her fingertips and fluttered them and her eyelashes coyly at Doc. She was giggling, though the glass door was thick enough to prevent his hearing it.

Millie stepped to the door carefully, as if she were picking her way through a flower bed—Doc's apprehension grew. She regarded him through the glass. Her eyes, since she'd been taught by Celia to pencil sunburst streaks all around them, reminded Doc of daisies. At the moment, however, she seemed unable to focus. Finally she undid the latch and slid the door aside.

She said, "Well, my dear, it's about time you showed up." Her speech was as deliberate as her steps had been. "Well, don't just stand there with your mouth open. Come in, come in."

She ushered him in with a flourish, then retrieved her tumbler from the floor. She toasted him with it, spilling some amber liquid on her hand.

"Here's to you..." She drew a breath, rolled her eyes and tossed back the dregs in the tumbler. "... And all those bastards out there." She breathed sherry fumes at him.

How unbearably sad it was to watch Millie teetering and chortling like a drunken crone. He had feelings for her which he obstinately avoided analyzing. It was all he could do to admit that feelings existed. Was it reasonable to call what he felt for Millie admiration? Would he admit to a modest sexual attraction? If hard pressed—he would have to be very hard pressed— he might concede to call it a chaste sort of desire. He would never admit to lust; he couldn't come to terms with lust, even the helplessly innocent lust of a second-grader for his teacher. Millie stirred him in ways he savored, feared and refused to understand.

At the moment, however, he was filled with remorse to see her diminish herself this way. He had to assume partial responsibility. Sandy would never forgive him.

Millie stuck out her tongue at him, but then shrugged and tried to pull herself together.

Doc said, "What's going on, Mil? Where's Celia?"

Instead of answering, she fluttered her eyelashes at him. Doc went to the small wet bar Sandy had built into one of the bookshelves. The brandy bottle was uncorked and nearly empty. Had she consumed that much? He lifted the bottle so she could see it. "Jeez, Mil."

"Help yourself, Sweetie, and freshen mine." Picking her way carefully again, Millie handed over her tumbler. She turned her attention to the La-Z-Boy, wondering if returning to it was worth the effort. Her decision made, she eased back into it, balancing her tumbler in the air, and returned the chair to an almost fully prone position with her skirt hiked way up again. She looked down at her exposed thighs, then at Doc; she giggled and nodded.

They silently stared at each other until Millie appeared to tire of the game. When creases appeared at the corners of her eyes and at the point of her chin, and her lower lip pushed into a pout, Doc thought she was finished with games and would finally cry.

Wrong. She didn't, and the tension between them grew. She said, "I hope you're not gonna just stand there in a snit." She pointed her right toe at the couch. When Doc didn't move she barked, "Siddown!"

The couch was much too near; Doc preferred to take a seat at a distance from Millie, out of reach of her tantalizing eyes and naked thighs.

But each time she aimed her toes at the couch, her skirt hiked up an inch. If he didn't move soon, he'd be able to see... He dropped onto the couch and tried to rivet his attention on her face.

"I'm not in a snit," he said, "honest I'm not. You just surprised me with the locked door and the...the drinking surprised me, that's all." He jerked his head toward the bar. "I never saw you so...Jeez, Mil, you drank a lot. I remember your telling me you hated sherry. You said it tasted like *Formula 44*."

No answer.

Millie had abandoned the conversation to measure the distance between her and the bar, wondering if she could make it for a refill. She shrugged hopelessly.

"Millie? You drank a lot, nearly a liter. Don't tell me no. I gave Sandy that bottle for his birthday; it wasn't opened until last weekend. It's almost empty now. You drank a liter."

"I did not."

She looked over at the bar but she had given up on the refill idea. She turned her face to the ceiling, her lips silently moving, as if a tally of the drinks she'd had was up there.

When she looked back at Doc she said, "I guess I did."

With pursed lips, knitted brow and hands folded in her lap, Millie proceeded to disapprove of herself severely. Another game—Doc sighed.

Millie said, the words tumbling out of her, "It really does…it has a lousy taste I never understood why you and Sandy like it…I told Ceilie I couldn't stand the smell…said 'Please don't ask me to take a sip not even one' but she insisted and I held my nose." She put on a Mr. Yuk face, with pinched nose and protruding tongue. Her eyes danced. She was obviously delighted by the face. "And I gulped it down and Ceilie forced me to take another."

In Millie's lap another game was underway, apparently without her knowledge: her fingers twined and intertwined in what looked like a game of cat's cradle, without string.

"The third swallow tasted pretty good I liked the fourth too and the fifth and sixth…."

Doc left the couch to kneel beside her and press her hands—they felt cold as ice—between his.

Now she was back to a wide-eyed pout. She cried, "Oh, Doc, those men were so mean. Why were they so mean?" A question he'd asked of Celia, so he didn't know the answer, but he knew who she was referring to. He clenched and unclenched his fists, wishing they were there now, to be punched.

"The fat one," Millie went on, "could hardly keep from laughing. He kept rocking back and forth, flapping his fat belly at me. He wasn't satisfied to tell me what happened to Sandy, the bastard wanted to beat me over the head with it. And that other guy, the one looks like a vulture?"

"Poke Perkins."

"Beady eyes and a mean mouth?" Hugging herself protectively, Millie watched Doc, waited for him to confirm that they were talking about the same person. And he did, not with words but by instinctively reaching for the lump behind his ear.

She said, "He was the one hit you? I should've known. He kept staring at my boobs. I thought he was gonna grab me. Just thinking of those eyes makes my skin crawl."

Millie fully righted the La-Z-Boy and asked to see his hurt place. "It hurts a lot, doesn't it? I won't touch it, I promise." Doc turned away. "Don't pull away, I can't see anything but hair." She caressed his neck with a gentle hand and her sherry breath. "Oh, dear, that looks awful. Are you sure you're okay?" Teacher sounded very pleased with her second-grader. "You're being very brave. Such a bad hurt and you didn't make a single complaint."

She fussed with his hair as she continued. "Somebody ought to do something about those two, they really hurt you. They did a job on me, too, shook me up pretty badly. By the time they left here I was in pretty bad shape. When Ceilie got here, I tried not to let it show, told her I was fine, but really, I was in bad shape."

Doc found it uncomfortable to listen to her. He expected to hear anger that would match his own, but instead he heard an odd mix of offhandedness and magic realism—teacher telling her second-grader that she'd found a troll living under a footbridge.

He squirmed.

"Be still!" she admonished, tapping his shoulder. "I talked to the nicest lady from the *Olde Posie Shoppe*. She was very sweet on the phone and she knows everything there is to know about ferns. And the man from the funeral home, Mr. Hanrihan? He said Sandy would get the best, English walnut I think he said, and brass…umm."

Doc couldn't bear her eyes; he looked away.

"The Rabbi called, too. Kaye, isn't it? I think that's what he said. Or was it Marx? No, that was his first name, Mark. Well, I'm not sure." Doc frowned; Millie giggled at him. "You never cared for him, did you? He was really very helpful. He promised to arrange everything at the cemetery. I was afraid to go out there, you know, to pick a place, but he, Rabbi Kaye, said we already had two places, all picked out and everything. Did you know Sandy had picked out two places for us to be…you know. Well, and Rabbi Kaye promised, well, he hoped to find lots of nice things to say about Sandy."

Doc found this chatter terribly upsetting. Her hands were folded in her lap with her head bowed over them. Should he try to stop her, Doc wondered, or was it better to let her run on, get it all off her chest? He didn't know what was best.

"I had a call from the *County Tribune*, wanting details for Sandy's obituary. I remembered the day he graduated law school and the day he opened the office in Sutersberg. And I had to call the director of Camp…um, that camp, Whatserface?"

She was unable to think of the name of the camp Ellie had been attending all week. Of course she couldn't, there was nothing between Millie and hysteria except a snoot full of sherry. Doc wondered if he ought to offer her more.

He said, "Wha-Nah-Hat-Chee. It's Camp Wha-Nah-Hat-Chee, Mil. Does somebody have to go get her? If so, I'll do it."

"The director is bringing her, he volunteered." She took a quick breath and exhaled just as quickly. "Poor Ellie, Thursday's her father's funeral. I arranged it all. Big deal!" Her lip went up in a sneer. "I'd hoped Celia or you, Doc, would be here to help me, but neither of you showed up."

Doc whimpered, "It's my fault, Mil, all my fault. I did everything wrong, made a damn fool of myself instead of coming here, as I should have."

"Forget it. You're here now, aren't you? It was a bad time but it's over with. Forget it." Millie pushed aside a few strands of chestnut hair that had fallen over her eye. "I was in bad shape, though, and you know you can't fool Celia about anything. She said I needed a sedative and she was right, but I didn't have a thing in the house. She remembered the doctor left pills for you for once you were over your concussion. She was gonna run home to get them, but I wouldn't let her go. The thought of being alone again…, I couldn't stand the thought." She drew several deep breaths, fighting back a giggle. "Ceilie was really furious at herself—you know how she can get—kept calling herself the stupidest person in the world for not thinking I might need one of those pills."

A sober Millie would've realized the futility of mimicking Celia, but now her eyes were bright with the idea.

She sucked in her cheeks and knitted her brow; it was a failed attempt to look thin and resolute. She also tried Celia's precise, theatrical way of pronouncing words: "Oh, damn! Damn me for a stupid so and so." Immediately she saw Doc didn't approve, so she dropped it.

She said, "Doc, lighten up. Don't you see how funny it is?" She puckered up and wagged her head.

Here comes Shirley Temple, he thought.

"Our Celia is so serious, oh, so serious. Hates inefficiency, she does, especially her own."

Doc didn't approve of Shirley Temple, either.

Millie replaced her imitations with a quick summary of events, ticking them off on her fingers: "One, Celia wanted to get those pills; two, I wouldn't let her go; three, she took the sherry from the bar and insisted I drink some; four, I did like she said, held my nose and drank some and felt better, just like she said I would. Guess I got used to the taste. I kinda like it now."

"But, Mil, where *is* she, where's Celia?"

She talked right over him. "What a restless night I had and—Jeez—I had the craziest dreams. Does sherry give you crazy dreams? But what a headache I had this morning. Took two aspirins and three more sherries to get rid of it. Hair of the dog, right, Doc?" Once again strands of hair fell over her eye; this time she blew air at them. Then something came to mind that left Millie looking misty-eyed.

She said, "I had a really nice dream about Sandy. You'd've enjoyed seeing him looking so happy, Doc. I hadn't seen him looking so happy in years. He was kinda fuzzy in the dream, like I was watching through a frosted window. But, oh Doc," she breathed, her hands clasped under her chin. "He was laughing out loud. Imagine that. He was sitting on the couch in his office, facing the private door. He was almost naked. All he had on were a white shirt collar—no shirt, just the collar. Isn't that silly?—and one of his brown neckties. Nothing else. Dreams are silly, aren't they?"

Doc wasn't sure but he nodded.

"Sandy was pointing his finger at someone. I couldn't see who it was because that someone, who-ever it was, had stepped beyond the door out of sight.

But somehow I knew it was a woman. Anyway, Sandy kept pointing at her and laughing."

Doc said, "That's the end? The whole dream?"

"I said it was silly, didn't I? Ceilie said so, too."

In the silence that followed Millie seemed to be daring him to comment; he refused to risk it. Pointing at his face she said, "You look as glum as Ceilie did when I told *her* about the dream."

"Listen here, Mil," Doc insisted. "Where's Celia now? I gotta know."

"Oh, she's gone." She walked her fingers through the air toward the patio doors. Doc's eyes followed them. "Hours ago. She was in a snit, went out of here with murder in her eyes." Millie looked at her wristwatch. "She must be murdering someone right about now, whoever he is.

"But don't worry," she said, "we've got plenty of time." With that she grabbed the kneeling Doc with both hands behind his neck and tugged him forward. "Plenty of time, she won't interrupt us."

Doc tried to escape her grasp; he couldn't, though he struggled to. He only succeeded in making things worse by pulling her out of the recliner and on top of him, with his face pillowed against her breasts.

They were firmer than he'd imagined, more resilient but just as warm as he imagined they'd be. He knew he ought to resist, but he felt himself yielding, letting go and pressing himself into her warmth.

Incredible warmth, incredible peace—his universe seemed to hold its breath.

Suddenly, however, the throbbing of Millie's heart intruded on the moment, changed it to one of panic as Doc felt himself engulfed, unable to breath. She was smothering him.

He squirmed roughly, regaining his balance and wrenched free of her.

He immediately turned his back so that Millie wouldn't see how aroused he was. With the back of his hand he wiped his mouth, and instinctively he touched behind his ear.

Millie's eyes mocked him. She said, "What's the matter, did I bump your hurt place? Or did I scare you?"

"Uh, no, I just couldn't...oh, never mind."

"Personally, I don't see any harm in a little affection between friends. Especially now, I could use a little affection right now. Any harm in it, do you think?"

Was there a safe reply? He doubted it. "Mil..."

"Damn you, answer me. Is there any harm in it?"

"Uh...well, no, I guess not."

It's the sherry, he thought. Really, it's the sherry. Sandy's not yet in his grave. It's the sherry.

"Then what're we waiting for?"

"The time's not right, Mil, what with Sandy... you know, and there's Celia to consider."

"**Fuck Celia!**" She leapt to her feet, staggered, then recovered and stamped on the floor. "**Fuck her, y' hear me**?"

Don't, Mil, he thought, *don't. Don't shout it in my face.* He felt dizzy, acid burned his throat and his mind screamed, *Hold your ears, Doc, hold them tight. You too, Sandy.*

"Celia's no better than all the rest of the goddamn bitches out there. She was fucking my Sandy. Oh yes, she was. Why shouldn't I, why…"

She fled the room wailing, "Oh, shiiiit!"

CHAPTER 16

John Grimes flipped the switch on his desk intercom. He asked his Aunt Maggie, "Any word yet from Pittsburgh?"

"Nothing yet, Johnny dear," Maggie Pedersen answered.

More often than he liked to admit, Grimes had found himself in agreement with the County Commissioners on budgetary matters. The VW Rabbit factory was down to running a single shift instead of its usual three, and many coal miners and steelworkers were laid off, probably for good.

These were lean times throughout western Pennsylvania, and Piazza County was no exception. A tight grip on the purse strings wasn't only a virtue, it was a necessity.

He agreed with the Commissioners, for instance: Piazza County needed its own Medical Examiner like it needed another pizza parlor. There were too few questionable deaths in the County to justify the cost. And, too, in spite of the fact that there was serious business to be done in the District Attorney's Office, Grimes was generally in favor of a relaxed, friendly atmosphere around the office. But maybe filling the position of private secretary with his maiden aunt had gone too far.

Damn all Commissioners and damn all budgetary constraints—he kicked his desk, not for the first time by the look of it. He was on pins and needles waiting on Pittsburgh's Medical Examiner—the snooty bastard—to submit his report on the death of attorney Sanford Klein. He was taking his good old time.

BZZZ!

"Whatsit, Aunt Maggie?"

"AnnaMae…er, Celia Goldenson is here, Johnny dear."

Muttering, he hustled to the door and got it open just in time to allow Celia, looking more than usually upset and determined, to blow past him. He was almost frozen in place by the rigidity of her posture. Jeez, he thought, is her dander ever up.

She took a seat and he hurried to his place across the desk from her. Confused, he attempted a nonchalant gesture toward the visitor's chair, which she already occupied. He also fumbled an attempt to keep his voice casual.

He said, "Well, ma'am. We've put aside pressin' matters but now…"

"Drop the phony Abe Lincoln crap, John." She dashed the words like icicles in his face. "I'm here on serious business. I'm here to stop the rumors about me and Sanford Klein and you're gonna help me. You damn well better. They're not true, dammit." There was a bitter twist to her mouth. "You and that, that Nuzzi person, the two of you have caused enough trouble. It's gotta stop."

She reminded Grimes of a cornered cat, spitting mad and sparking at the eyes—he gawked at her.

Celia mocked him by imitating his Aunt Maggie: "Did you hear me, Johnny dear?"

He felt his ears burn.

She examined his face and decided to change her tack. She allowed the icicles to melt from her voice. She said, "Maybe I was wrong. I hope I was. Unlike Sheriff Ianuzzi, maybe you don't get off on hurting people. Maybe. So I'll ask you nicely. Will you help me?"

Grimes lowered his eyes and pushed his chair back a few inches. He said, "Gee, Celia, I will if I can."

Celia watched him shy away. She said, "Listen here, John. The rumors about me and Sanford have got to stop. People, especially people I care about, are starting to believe them. They've got to stop. Now!" Leaning forward, she gave his desk a karate chop.

Grimes peeked down the low neckline of her blouse. What he saw down there kicked off a memory of his first pre-teen girlfriend in her very first bra—he sighed.

"Did you hear me, John?"

"Sure." Grimes took time to breathe. "But I don't see how I can stop rumors I didn't start. I looked into those rumors, sure, but I didn't start them. No ma'am." He kicked back even further in his chair. "I'd like to think what you say is true: no, I don't get my kicks from hurting people. Also no, I don't get my kicks from hurting good friends, like your husband, for instance. At the same time, it's not possible to stop an investigation just because somebody might get hurt." A thin smile and a shrug.

Celia eased back in her chair and crossed her legs. Grimes cleared his throat and continued, "Lookit. Say a guy is into some, shall we say, athletic activities? On his lunch hour." He paused in case there was an objection on Celia's part. There was none. "Big deal, right? Happens all the time, yes, even in Pizza County. Say right smack in the middle of athletic activities he up and dies. Again, big deal. I know he was Doc's best friend, but let's face it, guys his age take heart attacks all the time." Grimes nodded sagely and tugged at imagined chin whiskers.

"They're common as spots on a Hereford. So what's to be done? Simple. If I were the lady with him…" He paused, watching Celia carefully. "I would have called the cops. My boys would've looked things over real careful like, to corroborate her story. And if things looked, y' know, kosher, we would've played dumb. No publicity, no reporters, nobody the wiser. That's what I'd have done, if it was me. But this chick… You insist it ain't you?"

She replied cooly, "Right, I insist."

Grimes sighed. "So this chick remains anonymous. But, damn her, she flew the coop leaving us holding a sack of rotten eggs: a naked corpse and no corroborating witness. That means an investigation, an autopsy, reporters snooping round. The works. And everybody knows the Pizza County Coroner doesn't know his ass from…uh, pardon the French. Coroner Columbo is a pharmacist. Jeez, Celia, we had to send the body to Pittsburgh."

"You run a classy operation, Johnny dear."

Grimes wriggled uncomfortably in his chair. "The goddamn ME's keeping me waiting forever. That bastard does it on purpose, I swear." He raked his fingers through his hair. "I'm losing hair over this business. I'd gladly handle it quiet like, Celia, if only I had that woman to corroborate." He looked at her hopefully; she shook her head and he let it drop.

"But I don't have her. What I *do* have is a couple of cops who've been watching too much TV, and a good friend with a lump on his head, a Pittsburgh M.E. taking forever with the autopsy and a deceased who I can't remember what he looked like. But I don't have *her*. Jeez."

Grimes exhaled and seemed to deflate. "Help me, Celia, and I swear I'll help you." He held up his hand. "Honest Injun."

"Fair enough," Celia said; she glanced at her watch. "Do you have time for a long story?"

He grimaced at the phone and nodded.

Celia uncrossed her legs, cleared her throat and began:

"Two or three mornings in the last several weeks Sanford had stopped in to talk—just to talk. That's got to be how the rumors got started, one of the neighbors must have seen him arrive after Jack left for the office." She paused, waiting for it to dawn on Grimes who Jack was. "Before the first time he showed up I had mostly ignored Sanford. He was Jack's friend and Millie's husband, that's all. Millie and I hit it off immediately, just like sisters, but Sanford..." She shrugged. "...he was just there. But one morning he turned up on my doorstep looking, I swear, like a lost puppy."

CHAPTER 17

That previous Spring morning, Celia said, continuing her narrative to John Grimes, she had awakened in a rare—for her—un-ambitious mood, not a good mood to take to her sales reps in the southwest cut of her *AnnaMae* territory. Which was why she was still in nightgown, robe, and slippers when there was a hesitant knock on the front door. Celia cursed. It was too hesitant a knock to be a professional salesperson—no one knew that better than Celia. And it wasn't a neighbor lady making a social call—Sutersberg ladies didn't chit-chat with Celia Goldenson. And it wasn't the right season for Girl Scout cookies. She guessed it was one of the high school's Marching Band Mothers.

"Take a morning off once in a blue moon," she muttered as she headed to answer the door. "That's when some woman shows up to sell you a hoagie." She yanked open the door. Sanford stood there with his hands in his pockets, gazing at the doormat. Celia stared at him; he fidgeted as if he had to pee.

She demanded, "Well, Sanford?"

Except for an *uh* and an *er*, Sanford was silent.

Celia had heard rumors about Sanford, but she thought a guy who stammers at a woman's door wasn't likely to be a womanizer. But she also knew if she smelled smoke there was liable to be fire. She poked at him with a slipper-ed foot.

"Sanford?"

He said, "I couldn't go to work today, couldn't face the four walls. Just couldn't."

Celia undoubtedly felt the way Sanford looked. The air around them both was heavy with inertia. She roused herself and was about to close the door on him.

He said, "I know you don't like me."

She denied that, hoping not to sound too defensive: "Well…no, I like you well enough."

"You don't have to deny it, I know I'm not…well. Millie and Doc are likeable, everybody likes them. And you…well, but me." He rubbed the side of his head with his shoulder. "You don't have to like me, I'd rather you didn't, actually. When I saw your car in the driveway…You're usually off somewhere by now. I can't believe my luck, but there's the Anna-MaeMobile and here you are. I thought I'd stop in."

Because Celia was in no mood for work didn't mean she was in a mood for him. She snapped at him, "Oh? A little surprise visit?" She took him by the chin, roughly forcing eye contact. "I've heard all the rumors about you. Did you come sniffing around here to get laid? The truth, now."

# # #

Grimes blinked in disbelief. "You said that to his face? It must have knocked him on his ass."

"I wish. What he did, he started to cry. It made me feel like two cents. I wasn't trying to hurt him, I only wanted to discourage him. I just wasn't in the mood for company, that's all. Well, I couldn't send him away with tears in his eyes, could I? So I sat him down on the back porch and went to make coffee."

# # #

After two cups of Celia's strong coffee Sanford stopped snuffling. He said, "I'm sorry, Ceil, I didn't mean to cry. I'm just what you needed today, right? I didn't plan it, I swear. How could I, you're never home mornings."

She tried to remain skeptical, but it wasn't easy to maintain any attitude in the face of his blandness.

After a pause he blurted out, "I'm in trouble, Celia. Bad trouble. With my practice and with Millie." He hung on that for a moment, as if mentioning Millie's name had robbed him of breath. "I'm losing her, Celia. She's going to leave me."

Celia felt a migraine coming on, mostly because she had been straining to keep Sanford in focus. But she had heard what he said and she wanted to deny it. "Oh, I don't think so, Sanford. I spoke to her just the other night and she never said a word about leaving."

"Believe me, she's going to leave. It's my fault, I know, but I can't do anything to stop her." A puddle of tears had gathered on the fleshy ridge below his right eye; it teetered there momentarily, spilled over and down to his mouth.

Celia shivered. She could see his eyes looking like those of a wounded bird and she could see those tears. Sanford Klein wasn't invisible, after all.

Sanford wiped away a tear with the palm of his hand.

He had been wandering the morning-quiet streets of their Oak Hill neighborhood feeling like a rat trapped in a maze. He'd come to the conclusion that his only hope lay in spilling his guts to Celia and soliciting her help. With her help maybe he could save his marriage.

He said, "I can do without lectures on right and wrong. And as for talking to my good buddy Doc... well." He shook his head and watched Celia shake hers as well. He said, "I need a tough, practical person with influence over Millie. Who else but you?"

"But I don't even... I mean... I'm hardly your friend, Sanford. I've known you for some time, yes, but I've mostly ignored you, haven't I?"

"True, but it might help, actually. It might make it easier for me to talk to you. What have I got to lose, your high regard for me?" With palms up he shrugged. "What have I got to lose?"

Celia went on:

Sanford began his narrative with his and Millie's attempt to make a go of life in Pittsburgh, which he referred to as *The Big City*. The picture he painted was of two newly-wedded lambs surrounded by packs of slavering wolves.

And Sanford's attempt at making a living at law in Allegheny County was depicted as a daily dose of frustration and rejection, sounding like a child squirming to avoid his daily spoonful of cod liver oil.

He opened an office above a laundromat on Pittsburgh's North Side, two tiny roach-infested rooms and a closet-sized toilet. The rickety wooden stairway to his entrance door vibrated rhythmically whenever a certain combination of washing machines and dryers were operating at once.

Sanford furnished the office entirely from a nearby *Ikea*: a tiny desk, a filing cabinet, two hard chairs, a wastebasket and coat rack—all assemble-it-yourself stuff.

Sanford said, "It was an awful place, but all I could afford. Some months I couldn't afford that." He shrugged. "Millie taught second grade. Without her paychecks, we'd have been on welfare."

He told Celia about a few clients who typified his early practice. By this attempt at re-telling them to Grimes, Celia had forgotten most of the details, but she was able to remember what they—a clumsy longshoreman, a half-blind stumbling alcoholic, an injured prostitute, a naïve shopkeeper—what they had in common: weak cases and no money to pay a lawyer.

Sanford's narrative made Pittsburgh's North Side neighborhood sound like some place out of *Les Miserables*. But at the time Celia remained skeptical.

The Kleins—Sanford, Millie, and five-year-old Ellie—had happened upon Sutersberg three years before during a Sunday drive on the country roads east of Pittsburgh. They had wandered off the Turnpike and followed a winding, two-lane road that meandered through Piazza County. As they gawked at the rural scenes drifting by their car windows, they felt as if they had driven backward in time. They passed grazing livestock, cornfields and neat, clapboard farmhouses with chicken coops and corn cribs in the yards.

After a few miles on Route 66 the farmlands gave way to rows of three-story houses of weathered brick, wooden railings and porch swings. The country road became a street that climbed a steep hill. At the top, the street made its way between two sober adversaries—Blessed Sacrament Cathedral and the public high school, each building glaring disapprovingly across at the other. The Kleins crested the hill and coasted down the other side—there was Sutersberg:

A railroad bridge, and to the left and far below, an old passenger station and freight house guarding the tracks. On the right a low, modern building of cut stone—Temple Adath Israel. A courthouse with a mustard-colored dome. A wide intersection, Otterman and Main, with a bank on each of three corners and the New Courthouse Annex on the fourth. Red brick in stubby rectangles, mom-and-pop store fronts of turn of the century construction, gingerbread facades. *The Five 'n Dime, Gunderman's Department Store*, a Rexall drug, a hardware store that bore a family's name and smelled mustily of old men and floor wax, a bell that tinkled when the door opened.

Once it became clear that Millie and Sanford were unlikely to find anything resembling happiness in Pittsburgh, they remembered Sutersberg and Piazza County.

According to Sanford, things got off to a fair start for him and Millie in Sutersberg. He found a vacancy on the fourth floor of the *First National Bank Building*, bigger than his office in Pittsburgh and the rent was reasonable, the office was clean, the stairs didn't shimmy and there was an elevator. And Millie was crazy about the house they found on Green Orchard.

Not only did Millie love her house and yard, she loved the neighbors, too, and they loved her. Unusual for Pizza Countians, who take after New Englanders in their reticence. If they have their druthers, they druther wait a while to give Pizza County time to rub the newness off a stranger. No hale fellow newly met for them. But after the stranger finds his place—or the County folks put him or her in their place—then folks feel right about acknowledging a stranger's presence. They trill offhandedly, "How do!" as if they were an old friend who'd been away and had just returned, as they'd always known they would. But that hadn't worked with Millie. She had charmed the neighbors out of their country reticence and made friends quickly.

But poor Sanford. For him the move changed nothing. His Sutersberg practice, like the one in the big city, was an immediate failure. Though he attended all of the Bar Association meetings, he made no friends among his professional colleagues. When he applied for a position with the Public Defender's Office, his application was mislaid. When he paced the Courthouse halls and haunted the hospital emergency rooms, no one noticed—he was invisible.

However the move to Sutersberg had indeed brought about a change, for the worse. Celia said, "Out here they didn't completely ignore Sanford as they had in the City. Out here they gave him a nickname."

Celia aimed ice daggers at Grimes. She said, "Damn you, John, and damn all the rest of you, too. Those nicknames you stick on people aren't funny. They're hurtful."

"Now whoa up, Celia," Grimes drawled. "I admit folks around here have been pretty rough on Klein—all that Invisible Man business. But we meant no harm, really we didn't, and I doubt it caused any."

"You don't call a man's dying harm?" Celia saw him wince; she inclined her head. "I'm sorry, that wasn't fair. But Sanford couldn't make a living. He had more trouble here than in the 'burgh. How was he supposed to pay the rent? He had a family to feed, a mortgage to pay, just like all of us *visible* people. How could he make it, with only one friend in the whole world—God bless my husband—and no clients or any hope of getting any? His situation was desperate.

Chapter 18

It was late afternoon and Celia, sitting across the desk from Grimes, cast a long shadow across the office floor. She looked at her watch, saw how late it was getting and decided to change her tack. She decided to skip over how Sanford tried his hand at every aspect of legal practice and how he had failed. *Tempus fugits*. It was time to tell Grimes about Sanford's very first success as a lawyer in Sutersberg—his first divorce case.

As Sanford began talking about his client, he tried to use Jane Doe instead of the client's real name—a gesture to client confidentiality—but it became clear at the outset that his client was someone Celia knew.

She said, "It was someone you've known all your life, John, a Pizza Countian born and bred. A natural beauty, I mean a looker. Thirty-five years old, small and blond with wide, innocent blue eyes. But tough. She has a kind of hardboiled mouth, if you know what I mean."

Grimes had to laugh. "Lonetta? That sounds like Lonetta Pagano. She was Lonetta Bortz then. Know what they used to call her in Sutersberg High?"

"I don't know and I don't want to know, thank you. Anyway. Yes, it was Lonetta Pagano. She was Sanford's first divorce client. Her husband, Joe, owns that shoe store."

Celia could see Grimes's feet through the well of his desk. "It wouldn't surprise me to learn you bought those black beauties you're wearing at his place on Pennsylvania Avenue."

Lonetta wanted to divorce her habitually unfaithful husband. She told Sanford at the time of their first interview that she wanted him to sue the bastard for everything he had, including his store full of smelly f'en shoes.

Sanford said to Celia, "To hear it now, she sounds like a real bitch. She is, for sure, a true bitch on wheels. But her husband is no better. Did I mind? Hell no. She was a real client, she could pay my fee. I really earned my fee, too, focused my entire attention on Lonetta's case." His mouth turned down. "I didn't have any other work to do. Anyway, I paid a man to follow Joe, and soon after I did that I knew I was going to win for Lonetta; I was not only gonna get his shoes, I was gonna get his socks, too.

"Joe told Lonetta he was putting in fourteen, fifteen hours a day in the shoe store. When he'd come home at night he was too exhausted to…well, perform his husbandly duties. But my man followed him and, sure enough, Joe had a little something going on the side. I went back and forth on the phone with Joe and his lawyer, and in no time I had arranged a sweet settlement for Lonetta."

Sanford made an appointment with Lonetta to tell her the good news. But the moment she was ushered into his office, he knew something was wrong: she was dressed carelessly, and her makeup was sloppily applied and streaked with tears. And something had changed about the way she looked at him. In their previous meetings she had seen him but hadn't seen him. Like everyone else, she had looked at him and had seen right through him.

"All of a sudden she wasn't looking at me in the same old way, as if I weren't there. She was actually seeing me, not seeing through me," Sanford said, "and I think it startled her to discover that I was actually a man. As if I'd grown a beard. I'd become a man and she became a woman with no self-esteem. She must have felt like a lump, a zero, no woman at all.

"I said a lot of things, trying to be supportive. Platitudes. If you haven't guessed, I'll admit I'm no psychologist. I figured, maybe if I spoke to her as if I were her big brother... Maybe all she needed to know was that somebody cared. I was half right, Celia, half right. What she really needed was to be cuddled.

"All of a sudden I felt my ass come out of the chair. I couldn't believe it myself, but everything important to me, my reputation, my ethics, even my marriage, had become meaningless. There was only Lonetta and her need. I found myself lifting her out of her chair, touching her, fumbling with her clothes. We were…we, well, right on the carpeted floor."

Afterwards, if Sanford is to be believed, Lonetta dressed herself and hurried out, with her back straight, head high, looking all together like a new woman. Sanford was still on the floor with his pants around his ankles and his shirt a tattered rag.

With a frown and a shake of the head Celia said, "I can just picture him lying there dazed but happy—he'd been needed."

Celia saw that Grimes had been affected by her story, but she wasn't sure how. Was he merely titillated? Or had she been believed?

Grimes had heard more than his share of scatological stories—how could he not have, glad-handing as he did around the Courthouse all the time. But told so bluntly by a woman? Uh uh. He found speech difficult.

He rasped, "Jeez, Celia. Jeez."

CHAPTER 19

Celia resumed telling Sanford's story at a point later that same afternoon after the so called "meeting" with his client Lonetta Pagano:

Sanford drove home overcome with weariness and barely able to turn the wheel of his car. The two steps up from the garage to the mud room seemed incredibly steep. His hand shook so badly he was hardly able to get the door open. When he finally managed it, he found little Ellie, then five years old, watching Mr. Rogers on TV and dutiful Millie setting the table for dinner. He couldn't answer the greeting Millie sang out—words stuck in his throat like wads of dry leaves. He was afraid to face her, thinking she would see guilt hanging from him like dead vines.

But no. They both rushed to him, Millie to take his coat, ease off his shoes, massage his neck and Ellie to climb up on his lap for a hug. But there was no comfort for Sanford Klein; in fact, their ministrations had the opposite effect. In Sanford's words: "The more they tried to comfort me, the more their efforts galled me."

\# \# \#

John Grimes tugged sagely at his chin, nodded and said, "That boy had a bad case of the guilts. Like poison ivy, scratching doesn't help."

Celia bridled at the interruption. "That more of your homespun wisdom, John?"

"Sorry."

Celia inclined her head in concession.

She said, "But I have to admit, you're right, he had a bad case of the guilts. And judging by the way it devastated him, I imagine in the same way he'd never felt useful before, he'd also never ever felt guilt before." She shrugged. "So he told Millie all about the meeting with…her, with Lonetta."

Grimes said, "Jeez. I imagine what followed the confession was a battle royal?"

Celia shook her head. "You'd think so, it certainly was what I expected to hear. But no. According to Sanford, that's not what happened. What happened was worse than that."

Sanford told Celia that he pleaded with Millie to shout at him, crying that the silence was destroying him.

No, Millie cried to herself. No sound, no tears, as if she had dried up inside, but what she did, she pulled Ellie to her and cupped her hands over Ellie's ears.

"You know what she was doing?" Sanford said to Celia. "She was covering Ellie's ears so she couldn't hear what a rat her father was."

Sanford wanted to die, he wanted to dry their tears, but there weren't any. He wanted to run and not run, both. But horrible as the outcome was, confessing it was the bravest thing Sanford Klein had ever done.

#　#　#

Celia said to Grimes, "After skewering him with silence for a couple hours, Millie…well, I'm not sure what she did, although Sanford told me she forgave him. Can infidelity ever be forgiven? Not if you ask me, but maybe Millie did, maybe she forgave him. But she also made him promise that it wouldn't happen again. And he did, he swore up and down that it wouldn't. Sanford told me he meant to keep his word. I'm not sure I believed him."

Grimes said, "Maybe he intended to, who knows? You know how that kind of thing goes."

#　#　#

In the face of events, his intentions were moot—*res ipse loquitur*, as Sanford himself was fond of saying. Lonetta Pagano placed one of Sanford's business cards in the detergent-reddened hands of every disgruntled Pizza County woman she met. One after another of them became Sanford's clients. Each one of those relationships followed a pattern that was perhaps different in one detail or another, yet each one was the same as a single jellybean in a bagful. Each client had eventually needed to be cuddled, and who was on hand to do the cuddling but Sanford Klein? Each of his lapses was followed by an attack of remorse, a scene in which he confessed, Millie wept and covered Ellie's little ears, and finally after a renewed promise that it wouldn't happen again, a reluctant reconciliation.

Grimes said, "What did Lonetta see in that...that non-entity of a man?"

"How should I know?" She shrugged. "Whatever it was she saw, she wasn't alone. What did any of the other women see in him? Hell if I know. But I know others called and kept calling. He was too desperate to say no. I believed him when he told me that he didn't mean to break his word to Millie."

"Let's see if I've got it straight, Celia. Here's this guy, Sanford Klein. An Invisible Man, fer Chrissake. Divorces are his ruination and he knows it. He can't resist the temptations, can't handle the guilt. In all fairness to the wife that he loves and the little kid that he adores, he's gotta turn divorces down. But they're the only thing he can get and the only thing he's any good at. Jeez, Celia, talk about being stuck between a rock and a hardon. Excuse my French."

Celia showed him her teeth. "I'm gonna let that pass." But with a snarl.

She took a breath to calm herself before going on. "As I said earlier, I was anything but Sanford's friend, but I ended up on his side. Can you believe it? Me?" She tapped herself on the chest. "Millie's friend, practically her sister? He came to me to talk about hurting her, and all I could think of was, what could I do to help him? But he was so damned miserable sitting there with his chin in his hands and weeping. He was in hell, John, really in hell, and their marriage was in a wretched state."

Grimes scratched his right sideburn and scowled at his watch. He excused himself for interrupting, pressed an intercom key and spoke at it, "Aunt Maggie, that call to…"

"Nothing yet, Johnny dear."

His ears reddened; Celia tried not to laugh. She grinned but kept quiet.

Grimes watched her closely, as if she were on the stand. "Klein wasn't trying to get you to speak for him, intercede with her?"

"That's what I suspected, too. But no. Actually he wanted me to stop speaking to her. I'd been urging Millie to leave him."

Grimes started to interrupt, but changed his mind.

"He asked me, begged me actually, to either help him or stop working against him. Well, I did. After his visit that morning, I decided to try to help him. I changed my tack with Millie—without telling her about his visit, of course."

She paused. "I wonder if that was a mistake. Anyway, I told her I'd changed my mind, that maybe she'd better stick with Sanford, after all. I said he was probably a decent enough sort, no better and no worse than most. I said, 'Mil, you ought to try and work things out.'"

Her shoulders sagged. "I don't think it did any good. In fact I'm sure it didn't. And to make matters worse, I'm afraid Millie and my Jack are starting to believe those rumors about Sanford and me."

Grimes felt they had finally reached the perfect point to ask the sixty-four-thousand-dollar question: "Did Klein ever drop a hint, ever mention any names? Y' know, who the latest divorcee was?"

"What's the difference who it was? All this snooping. God, John. Just to satisfy your curiosity?" He cocked his head to one side. "Surely it can't make any difference? There's no question that he died of natural causes. There's no question, is there John?"

Grimes rolled his eyes in a plea to heaven. "Oh but there is. An empty pill bottle they found in his washroom. We think maybe… and that damn City M.E.'s Office…"

Bzzz!

Grimes reached for the intercom box.

"Medical Examiner from Pittsburgh calling, Johnny dear."

CHAPTER 20

Doc felt trapped in the house. The walls were yammering at him, so he pushed past the screen door and trudged into the yard. His legs were rubbery and awkward, and his knees wobbled under his weight. He plodded to the back of the yard, where a lawn swing was sheltered in the shadow of a large maple. On a normal day—he sighed, wondering if normal days were a thing of the past—he might have found Celia on the swing. It was her habit to retreat—his word, not hers—to retreat there to wrestle with business problems. It had often amused Doc to watch from a distance as Celia, with furrowed brow and a stern set to her mouth, would scold the tree trunk for having blown an *AnnaMae* cosmetics sale. She had always insisted that her problems could be seen with a fresh perspective and a solution found in that quiet, shady place. It had always worked for Celia; now, sagging into the swing, Doc hoped it would work for him.

There was a stale, dry taste to the air. How long since it had rained? He shrugged and let his weary eyes roam around the yard. The grass, which he usually kept trim and straight as a military haircut, had grown uneven and the tips of the blades were brown. The mountain laurels drooped, as did the azaleas, and singed, yellow petals lay in curled heaps beneath the forsythias. The barberry hedges were thorny green as ever, but they too looked as if they had been through a recent struggle. Without his having noticed it, Spring had come to a sudden end. He'd neglected his yard at a crucial time.

The yard had always been a comfort to Doc. The predictable way in which it changed with the seasons soothed and reassured him. When the flower beds had been weeded and raked, when the hedges had been trimmed, the grass had been mowed and the borders edged, he felt that not only the yard but his entire life had been put in order.

He liked things to be tidy, a trait inherited from his mother, or so he supposed. Yes, he was like his mother that way. Pizza Countians joked that soon as Doc Goldenson got your teeth fixed up, you could go ahead and eat off his office floor. According to Patsy Policastro, his assistant, Doc spent as much time tidying the office as he did fixing teeth. Doc himself admitted that, in his mind, he didn't so much restore his patients' mouths as clamber in there and tidy up. The house was Celia's domain—more's the pity. Thank God she left the yard to him.

He'd always kept his mind tidy, too—until now. He'd stood guard like a customs official at the gates of his mind, and examined methodically everything that sought entry. He would tidy things up and decide on a proper storage compartment before allowing anything to pass inside. There was a compartment for everything in Doc's mind: sights, sounds and other sensory perceptions each had one; sexual feelings, religious beliefs and political attitudes had compartments, too; he reserved one for things not well understood; even one for things he was powerless to do anything about. He'd taken pains to fit the compartments with steel lids, rubber gaskets and snappy hinges; that way, information wouldn't spill out and untidy his mind. As Doc's reputation for compartmentalizing became common knowledge in the County, some folks not so tidy of mind as he would laugh at what they thought was his naiveté. They were just jealous.

He stored gossip in a compartment labeled UN-PLEASANTNESS, after which he snapped the lid shut and the gossip was forgotten—no mean feat for Pizza County, where folks bragged that everyone knew what was going on in everyone else's bedroom. They meant, of course, everyone except Doc Goldenson.

"Jackasses," he muttered. Harboring gossip was no way to keep a tidy mind.

But now things were becoming less tidy by the minute. Not that he'd lost his talent for compartmentalizing, it was just that too much had been crammed into the one compartment. No matter how hard he mentally pushed down on the lid, unpleasantness leaked out.

Had something been going on between Celia and Sandy? Though John Grimes had hinted as much, Doc had neatly locked it away. And throwing a punch at Nuzzi, even if he had missed, had helped shrink the fat police chief's innuendoes to a tidy size. And Poke Perkins had pounded down the lid—with a blackjack. If only Millie hadn't blurted that accusation in his face—*She was fucking my Sandy*. Or words to that effect. That compartment was over-full and leaking.

He closed his eyes and concentrated on breathing deeply, trying to settle his panicky stomach. The walk to the Klein house and back had been a mistake. Clear as day in Doc's mind was a picture of Dr. Sam pointing a tobacco-stained finger at him and grumbling, *"Should've known I had a damn fool on my hands."*

With his eyes still closed, breathing deeply and evenly, he concentrated on sounds. A car, no, a van cruised along Peartree Way; a distant air conditioner clicked on, whined, fanned air. Nearer, little creatures hummed about their business: bees in the azaleas, ants on the peonies, beetles on the roses—Doc imagined he could hear them munching. A comforting sound. A comforting image: Doc, himself, listening to the munching of bugs instead of listening to the yapping of gossip. Not knowing.

A bee buzzed by Doc's ear on its way to the laurels. He had no fear of it; to his recollection he'd never ever been stung. Nor to his recollection had he ever had to question his wife's conduct. It surprised him, as a review of his life drifted by on currents of warm air, to realize how dependent on Celia he had always been. He relied on her earnings from *AnnaMae of New Rochelle* to supplement a small-town dentist's modest income. More to the point, he relied on her toughness and good sense—he wondered if he had any traces of these qualities himself. And until this moment he hadn't realized or admitted to himself that the tidiness of his life that he was so damn proud of depended not on a trait he'd inherited from his mother but on...what? Celia's honesty? Integrity? Fidelity? Yes, yes and yes.

What had she been up to for the last fifteen years while his back was turned? He'd never had to worry. He'd never been stung, so he had no fear of bees. But wondering about it now had untidied his mind.

CHAPTER 21

A car braked hard in the driveway—SQUEE! A dry brake pad at the right rear of the Anna-MaeMobile had been squeaking for weeks. Doc heard the car door slam and then the house door slammed.

"Jack? Jack?"

Various inner doors slammed as Celia searched the house. Doc became alarmed by the urgency in her voice. Finally she emerged onto the rear deck.

"Jack?" Celia stomped her foot. "Where in hell is that man?"

"Back here, Ceilie. What's wrong? Hey, back here on the swing."

She started toward him. The glare of the late afternoon sun seemed to impede her progress; the grass snatched at her heels and she stumbled. She looked pale. Doc wondered if what he saw on her face was guilt. As the sun was sinking toward the horizon, his heart sank with it.

The closer she came the more her distress alarmed him. He began to fantasize: Wouldn't it be something if she kept on trudging this way, but never quite arrived? She did, though. She reached the swing, drew a few quick breaths and was about to blurt—something.

Please don't, he wanted to shout. *Enough blurting for one day.*

It stopped her, though he hadn't uttered a sound.

"Jack, what's wrong? You don't look well." She sounded distant and tentative. "Where've you been? Not at the office, I'm sure. I told Patsy not to let you near the office."

Doc shook his head. His mouth felt as if it were packed with cotton rolls, his tongue felt pebbly. He said, "I didn't go far, just to Millie's, but I shouldn't have. The walk exhausted me." He felt vulnerable to Celia's searching eyes. "Millie was drinking Sandy's sherry and she was drunk. Oh boy, was she ever drunk and saying crazy things. She had no idea what she was saying. I won't hold her responsible for any of it."

Celia nodded and with a hand against her chest as if she were holding her heart in place, she appeared to fold her lean body accordion-like into the swing. The regret Doc saw in her eyes made him feel wretched.

While she mustered her resources, Doc stared glumly at his lap. She said, "Jack, whatever Mil said… Jack?" He was avoiding her eyes. "I can explain. Damn it, Jack, look at me!"

That sounded like the old Celia. Hopefully, he looked up at her. Except for a bead of perspiration on her upper lip, she looked cool and unaffected. She sat poised, submitting to his gaze with patience, even defiance.

He wondered if he had been wrong, maybe it wasn't guilt he was seeing. Sure, her eyes were moist as if she might have been crying earlier, but now they looked clear and open, not as if they were hiding anything. Damn it, they were chiding him, calling him a damn fool.

Her smile lines deepened. "What to say?" Her color heightened; she held eye contact. "Jack, no matter what you heard, no matter what, I can explain, I will explain." A definite smile now. "Later. But for now..." Doc was about to interrupt when she touched his lips with two fingers. "Don't say anything. Either the truth shows or it doesn't."

He continued to search her face. Her eyes wouldn't leave him alone. Their clarity, like newly-polished glass, insisted that he look right through to the inside of her. He did.

What a relief—he sighed, exhaling most of his weariness, and drew his first comfortable breath in hours. Its taste was exquisite.

"That's better," she said. Her hand was cool against his cheek. "You thought Sanford and I...well, I'm not surprised. You're such a dope." Her smile was almost demure.

Doc hadn't seen such a look on her face since... when? He rubbed his eyes and grinned.

Celia and Doc sat side by side on the swing; there was just enough room for them sitting side by side. Interrupted now and then by a bird's poignant comment, pausing occasionally to study an interesting cloud formation, looking deeply into each other's eyes when the telling reached an emotional highpoint, first one then the other sketched her and his day:

Celia began with the morning she spent with Millie, at the end of which Millie had dismissed her gruffly, with a pretense of fatigue.

"She was practically incoherent by then," Celia said, shaking her head.

Sympathy or disapproval, Doc wondered.

"That was some idea I had last night, forcing the sherry on her. She was still working on that bottle when I got there this morning. And high as a kite."

"High, nothing. She was snozzled."

Celia shrugged. "Who knows, maybe it's better she got it off her chest."

When it was his turn Doc told a version of his and Millie's afternoon encounter—a censored version, omitting the bare thighs and the wrestling match. Without them it was a dull tale until the end, when his repetition of Millie's drunken accusation made Celia wince.

But she dismissed it.

"Don't blame her, Jack. She was drunk."

"Even so." Looking at the sky, his voice drifted off.

"Poor Mil. She must think every woman in town was, you know, with Sanford. Jack?" Her eyebrows went up at his discomfort. "And you're not sure about me, are you? Well, listen here, damn you. The only thing Sanford got from me was advice." She frowned. "Not very good advice, I'm sorry to say. Mil was going to leave him, at least Sanford thought so. See, Mil knew what had been going on between him and his clients. She did, Jack, because he confessed it all to her. So he thought she was going to leave him, so he came to me to talk it over. Really to get me to stop encouraging her to leave him."

An ache insinuated itself between Doc's ribs, causing him to suck in noisily.

"Are you all right?"

He saw a cloud that resembled a man looking toward the east. Was it Sanford? He whispered to it, "You'd expect more loyalty from a friend."

"Really, Jack! You're acting like a child. You're furious, aren't you? Because Sanford didn't take you into his confidence, he didn't come to you for advice. For your information, Jack Goldenson, there are things in this world that root beer won't cure."

She touched his cheek. "I didn't mean…Jack? He thought I could influence Millie, that's why he came to me instead of you."

After thinking it over she added, "He might've been better off if he had come to you. I was no help at all. Only made things worse."

"Don't blame yourself. It was Sandy's fault, blame him." There was bitterness in Doc's voice; it was a new flavor for him that seemed to startle them both. "I mean it," he insisted. "Why blame yourself? The whole stupid mess was Sandy's fault. It was justice, his dying the way he did. To, uh, to hell with him."

Noticing her surprise, he shrugged.

She tried a smile, failed, and stared at her lap. "It's just not like me to fail." She smacked her knee. "But, damn it, everything I did was wrong. The advice I gave Millie, the so-called help I gave Sanford. All wrong. Things went from bad to worse, the rumors started and, well, you know that part."

He nodded. "So you went to see Farmer Grimes. How'd that go?"

"Not too badly. Of course he tried to get a confession out of me. Oh, you know, that I was Sanford's secret lover."

Doc muttered a curse; she dismissed it with a flap of the wrist.

"You can believe I straightened him out on that score. After that, he was cooperative enough. We have an understanding, he and I."

"Oh?"

"Umhm. He promised to keep it quiet, sort of.

See, he was waiting for a phone call from Pittsburgh. When it finally came…"

Doc waited.

There's something else, Jack, she wanted to say. Damn it, there's always something else. Celia wanted to say it and get it over with, but she held her tongue. The fatigue on her husband's face, the hangdog look of him, like a puppet with loose strings, told her that he'd endured his limit at the moment. Later, she thought. Later was soon enough.

She said, "Just a complication, dear. It'll keep."

## CHAPTER 22

I t was a breathless night. Anticipation hung in the air like a humid veil; it hushed the creatures of the night, making their sibilant murmurings sound like love songs. After Doc had placed a small table out on the deck, Celia had covered it with a damask cloth, placed on it two slender ivory candles in sterling silver holders and served a chef's salad in a cut glass bowl. Then she brought garlic toast on a walnut board and burgundy in crystal goblets.

The night was so still, the candle flames rarely stirred; when they did their reflections danced in the wine with seductive glimmers of silver, ruby and sapphire.

Doc resisted the temptation to speak, thinking a wrong word would shatter the spell. He wished the moment would last forever; wished, too, that Celia were as affected by it as he was. She had carefully planned the spinning of this romantic web, setting the table just so, calculating its effect. He didn't care if it was staged, he found it provocative. Filled with desire, he could hardly breathe.

TING!

They touched goblets, sipped their wine, searched each other's eyes, sipped again. The wine warmed his body, stirred him. The candlelight stirred, shone ruby in the wine, sapphire in her eyes. Celia was so beautiful, he ached.

Still he was aware of her guardedness. She was anxiously watching him; measuring him. And waiting. For what? He wondered without wanting to know.

"You look...jeez, Celia." His voice faltered. He wet his lips with wine and savored the shivers that passed in waves through his body from looking at her. He allowed his gaze to openly drift downward from her eyes, along her delicate nose to her broad mouth and lips, to her long proud neck. The hint of breasts beneath her blouse.

Time is a bigger fool than I am, he thought. She hasn't aged, she's still a Tech co-ed.

Celia shook her head. She said, "The last few days...sorry, I just can't seem to get in the mood."

"I know how you feel. I do too, like I've been punched in the stomach. You don't look it, though. You look beautiful, and I feel better just being near you. I love you. How long has it been since I said that? Too long. Y' know, it still feels good, being in love."

She nodded but didn't reply.

"Aw, cheer up, Ceilie. Nothing will bring him back. Let's try not to spoil the night." She tried a brave smile and failed.

"What is it, Ceil? You've kept me waiting for hours. Once and for all, say it and get it over with. Is it something John Grimes told you? C'mon, out with it." Doc surprised himself, sounding more confident than he felt.

A deep breath helped her get started. "Your friend Johnny Grimes was waiting for a call when I got to his office. From Pittsburgh, from the Medical Examiner's Office. He sent Sanford's...he sent Sanford to them, and they were taking forever with the autopsy report. Grimes was climbing the walls."

Celia went on, "I couldn't understand why he was making such a fuss. Nobody knew Sanford was alive when he was alive, so why make a fuss now that he's dead? People die of heart attacks every day, don't they? I mean, I didn't know..." She quit the sentence, seeming to run out of breath.

"Well?"

Suddenly he guessed, and his heart dropped through his diaphragm.

"It wasn't a heart attack, Jack. Sanford swallowed a bottle of pills. Seconals, little red capsules like the ones Dr. Sam told me not to give you till later. The ones they all prescribe for insomnia."

His ears buzzed and his mouth went dry. He reached for the wine, but changed his mind when he saw how badly his hand was shaking.

"B-but everybody said he was with a woman.

They were wrong? I knew it. I knew they were wrong. Sanford wouldn't…"

Celia compressed her lips and shook her head. That stopped him.

"They don't think Sanford was expecting her, whoever she was. There were no appointments on his calendar. Whatshername, Helga something? The Nazi secretary?"

"Miss Shumacher."

"That's her. According to her, Sanford didn't have any appointments for the rest of the day. Grimes thinks whoever Sanford's visitor was, she walked in unexpectedly, right after he had swallowed the entire bottle of Seconals. She couldn't have known he'd taken them. They were doing it, you know, when the pills took effect. She would have had no warning."

Celia's mascara began to smudge. "His heart would've just…" She inclined her head and shrugged. "Just stopped."

CHAPTER 23

No sooner had the words left Celia's lips than they landed on ears that were afire with guilt. Now Doc not only knew he had failed his friend, but he knew when he had failed him: it had been the previous Friday afternoon. The thought nagged at him that if he'd been a wiser counselor, Sandy might still be alive. Last Friday.

He should've been more alarmed by the urgency in Sandy's voice when he'd called for a meeting at the root beer barrel.

He should've been more sensitive to the warning note in his friend's voice. Instead Doc felt he'd failed Sandy. Had Sandy's tendency toward invisibility somehow confounded him? There was no point in berating himself, but still…

The phone call had come to the dental office shortly before two o'clock last Friday afternoon. There was something unexpected in Sandy's normally insipid voice that Doc now realized was panic. Whispering into the receiver which he cupped with his fingers to avoid being overheard by Patsy and the patient seated in the operatory, Doc tried to calm his friend.

"Get hold of yourself, Sandy. I can't run out on Gordy Conklin. He's in the chair with a mouth full of impression paste. Yeah, yeah, a new set of dentures. Okay, look, I'll meetcha at the barrel soon as I can get away."

When Doc arrived at the *Five 'n Dime*, he found Sandy drumming impatiently against the barrel with unsteady fingers, and with a half-empty mug in his other hand. Next to him, an empty stool and a full mug waited for Doc. He took his place without a word of greeting, took up his root beer and blew off what was left of the foamy head. Sanford didn't acknowledge Doc's arrival, but the impatient drumming ceased.

Doc had decided to wait until his friend was good and ready to talk, but when Sanford spilled root beer on the counter and on himself, he changed his mind.

"What the hell, Sandy," he said. "Your hand is shaking."

"I'm...scared." Sanford exhaled in relief, as if saying the word had robbed it of its power over him. "Lookit," he said, displaying both hands, "scared shit-less."

Doc tasted his root beer and whispered into his mug, "Scared of what, Sandy? Open up, will ya?"

Sanford leaned toward him and apologized. "Forgive me, I didn't mean to make you wait. I nearly killed myself this afternoon." Doc nearly fell off his stool. Sanford held thumb and forefinger in front of Doc's face, the digits nearly touching. "I was that close to going out of my office window. Doc? Did you hear me? I nearly killed myself." One of Sanford's Cheshire-Cat grins failed to hide his fear, a hint of which could be seen despite the dullness of his eyes and heard in the slight quaver in his voice. Its sourness could even be smelled on his clothing. The impulse to back away from him was strong.

"I saw three clients this morning," Sanford said. "Jan...uh, one a woman whose husband is trying to punish her by forcing her into poverty. The other two are trying to hold on to custody of their children. A morning with the walking wounded. Know how a morning like that leaves me? I felt as if I was shriveled like a prune. I felt old and dried out, like a goddamn prune."

He made a vague gesture with his slight shoulders, not quite a shrug. "Those women are hurting, Doc, really hurting. They try to hide it, sure, and some of them put on a pretty good front. You'd think my office was the supermarket or a hair salon, the way they come breezing in, cool as a cucumber and brave as hell. But sooner or later they tear the wounds open right in front of me, and it makes me feel desperate, so goddamn desperate, but I can't get over the feeling of helplessness.

"It was late," Sanford said, talking to his mug of root beer. "It must've been around one o'clock before I had a minute to myself. I remember Miss Shumacher returning from the *Tearoom*, so, yes, it was around one. I plopped down at my desk with the sandwich and apple that Millie had packed in a brown bag." He looked up at Doc, the corners of his mouth moving into a questioning smile. "She packs me a lunch every day, you know." Doc frowned. "I felt drained, too tired to be hungry but too restless to just sit there. I went to the window, raised the venetian blind and looked out. I remember staring down at the people. Up and down Main Street people were walking, in and out of *Salerno's*, crossing the street, climbing the Courthouse steps. Fascinating, you know? How you can hypnotize yourself by staring at something for a long time?" He looked up at Doc. "I found it fascinating. I noticed that from the fourth floor of the *First National Building*, pedestrians were too big to be ants yet they were too small to be real people. They looked like toys.

"I don't remember opening the window and I don't remember putting my leg out. Just all of a sudden there I was, staring down at the street admiring the mechanical men, with my foot on the sill. Doc? On the windowsill."

The air around Sanford seemed too thin to inhale. There was an ache beneath Doc's breastbone, and his voice sounded reedy and echoing, as if it were sliding along the walls of a tunnel. "You you you really meant to jump? Out out out the window?" He squinted, shook his head and snatched a gulp from his mug. "Christ, you've got me shaking now. Jeez, are you all right now?"

"I feel fine now." After thinking a moment he said, "As a matter of fact, I felt fine then, too. I just couldn't stop shaking." He leaned to whisper in Doc's ear. "And I wet my pants. I backed away from the window all dizzy and scared and pissed all over myself."

Sanford looked greatly troubled as he searched Doc's face. He said, "Sorry to burden you with this, Doc."

Then suddenly Doc thought he knew what was really troubling Sanford, he felt he could read Sanford as easily as a banner headline on the front page of the *County Tribune*. For a man so perplexed by what he'd just been told, Doc thought his mind was functioning with remarkable clarity; he'd never been more intuitive in his life. He wasn't absolutely positive, and until he *was* positive he decided he needed to slow things down. This discussion was moving too quickly. His intuition was signaling, delay, delay.

"No, damn it," Doc declared. He slammed his fist on the counter in a mock display of indignation, a move he immediately regretted because of the attention it drew to them from other customers and the way it seemed to confuse Sanford. "You're no burden to your best friend, don't ever think that. For Chrissake, Sandy, what're friends for if you can't say what's bugging you? Whatever it is, y' hear?" Then he dismounted his stool. "We'd better leave, get you some dry pants."

Though he nodded absently, Sanford waited to be led. When he was finally on his feet, Doc examined his pants. The upper part of the left leg was a lot darker brown than the right, but he whispered, "It's not too noticeable."

"Nobody notices the Invisible Man." Sanford tittered.

Once outside neither man initiated any further discussion; it would have required shouting over traffic noise. They headed for Doc's car.

Doc suspected he knew the cause of Sanford's distress, but he delayed confirming it until he had cleared southbound traffic, then he said, "You had a fight with Millie, didn't you? Finally, after twelve years of marriage?"

Sanford, his chin pressed morosely to his chest, moved his head in a barely perceptible nod.

Doc felt a ten-ton weight lift off his shoulders. Now he was sure. He said, "The two love birds finally had a fight. But Sandy, you've told me a hundred times, '*We never fight, we're too much in love. Mil and I couldn't bear it.*' Isn't that what you told me?"

Sandy replied with a grunt, then took a hankie from his pocket to dab his damp eyes. "I told you that, and I meant it. We hadn't ever fought, not until last night. We've disagreed plenty of times, but one of us always backed off; sometimes me, sometimes Mil, but somebody always did. Until last night."

Doc saw his friend's lower lip quiver.

"What a fight we had. Really it was a battle. Everyone on Green Orchard Lane must've heard it. What a doozy of a fight. We must've been saving it up our whole marriage long."

Doc squeezed his friend's left shoulder in a way he hoped was reassuring. "It's not the end of the world, old buddy. What's the big deal about a married couple having an argument? We all have them. And yes, sometimes they are real doozies. It's normal.

"Just wait till we get you home, you'll see. Millie will be just as upset as you are; she's probably been fretting all day long. Her eyes will be all red from crying, and she'll be as anxious to make up as you are. Don't be so negative, Sandy," Doc said, now very sure of himself. "Believe me, it'll be okay."

Doc blustered on, "Who's the expert on women around here, anyway? Aren't there times when Celia and I put on the gloves? She's got an iron will, my Ceilie. I let her have her way most of the time. That's the way a man of experience handles it, Sandy." Sanford looked dubious. Doc added, "Of course there are times when I have to let her know who's boss."

"Huh." Sanford watched the Oak Hill Plan go by on his right. He said, "You passed our turnoff, boss."

Doc continued south without comment, hoping Sanford would fill the silence with his own talk. He didn't want to pry into what they had fought about, but…

Sanford volunteered, "I hardly know what set it off…well, I know what set it off, really, but I wasn't saying anything I hadn't said a dozen times before. And suddenly it came like a bolt of lightning. As usual I was telling Mil about my day. I always tell her what clients were in the office and…uh, exactly what was said and done. It helps keep my head straight, y' know? Next thing I knew—bam! Like a bolt of lightning she was all over me, shouting, stomping her feet, waving her fists. Can you imagine Millie waving her fists? But she was, waving her fists and telling me, no, demanding…"

"What, for Godsake?"

Sanford's lower lip threatened to pout. "That I stop, uh, handling divorcees."

Doc silently wondered at that. He agreed, divorce cases were distasteful, but everyone's work had distasteful aspects. Wasn't dental work distasteful to Celia? That deserved a vehement head waggle. But would she tell him to stop? Close up the office? Hell, a guy has to make a living.

Aloud he said, "I can understand Millie not wanting to hear about all those unhappy women. What could be easier? Stop telling her. Talk about something else, like for instance, what you had for lunch."

"She already knows what I had for lunch. She packed it, remember?" Doc waved an impatient hand. "Talk about the weather, baseball, anything, for Chrissake. Just don't depress her with talk about divorces."

Sanford lowered his head mournfully. "She's not depressed, Doc, she's convinced they're destroying me. She says… Hell, I'm not making myself clear. Those women, my clients, they're emotional wrecks. They're scared, confused. They feel cut up, as if their husbands cut them up and threw the pieces in the trash. They need to get those pieces back, Doc. They need to feel loved." He shrugged again.

"Well?" Doc made a right turn, beginning a loop that would bring them to Oak Hill by a series of old farm roads. "Well, okay, your clients are needy. I get it. But so are mine. A person with a toothache isn't needy?"

"You can fix a toothache, Doc. My clients need more than words can fix. More than I'm able to cope with, if you believe Millie."

Nothing more came from him until Doc, feeling himself being studied, turned to face Sanford's pathetic eyes.

Sandy said, "I try very hard to help them, very hard. Millie thinks I'm using myself up. Last night she compared me to a dollar bill. She said I was spending myself too fast and all that was left of me was a dime and a few pennies."

Doc insisted, "Millie wouldn't say that, Sandy. Never. Celia would say it, yes, but not Millie." Celia had been putting words in Millie's mouth, he was sure of it. She was sticking her nose in where it didn't belong.

Sanford shook his head. "No. I think you might be wrong on that score, Doc. I doubt Celia had anything to do with it. Millie's been harping at me for some time now to give up divorce cases and get back to other kinds of law practice."

Doc accelerated to climb Hillcrest Road, the rear entrance to the Oak Hill Plan. He said, "I don't know, pal. You don't impress me as the type to handle criminals."

"You've been watching too much TV, Doc. Not every criminal lawyer is a *Perry Mason*. There aren't many of those around, believe me."

Thinking of the lawyers among his friends who lunched at *Salerno's* every afternoon, Doc thought maybe Sandy was right. "Well," he said, "if Millie would prefer that, why not do it? Why bother with a lot of weepy women when you could be handling business law, or estates or even criminals?"

"Wish I could, but..." Sanford shook his head. "I tried that in Pittsburgh and I tried it here in Sutersberg. No go. I was a misfit in criminal law, in corporate law, in tax law. My clients, the few I had, didn't trust me and I couldn't blame them. From one time they saw me to the next, they didn't recognize me. I'm the Invisible Man, remember?"

Doc felt a sinking in his stomach that he tried to relieve by gulping air and rubbing his forehead.

With a faintly quizzical expression Sanford asked, "You're embarrassed? Why should you be, I could care less what I'm called."

"I don't like it, Sandy, and I won't hear it even from you. My best friend isn't invisible. There's more to see in him than, than… If only they took the trouble to look."

For a time Sanford was silent. He seemed too weary to reply or even to focus his eyes in Doc's direction. He did so almost dreamily before whispering, "Thanks, pal. I like you, too." Uncomfortable, both men looked away. Sanford said, "Truth is, I failed in the 'burgh because I kept trying to be somebody I wasn't. I won't go back to that. Everyone needs to feel useful; I certainly do. If my clients want an invisible man, well, hell, what else can I do, anyway? That's what I am."

Sanford lifted his chin and looked around. "Why aren't we moving?" They were parked in front of his house. "I didn't realize," he said and climbed out of the car.

Doc said, "I still say that bit about change for a dollar is from one of Celia's cosmetics sales pitches. Don't you think…" He let it go as Sanford wandered off across the lawn to his front door.

At the time, Doc felt he had succeeded in putting the war between the Kleins in perspective and the nearly fatal incident at Sanford's office window was, rather than an intentional act, merely an accident, a mishap even. And the fact that they had had a doozy was no reason for further intrusion on his or Celia's part. But now he couldn't help feeling that if he'd been a better counselor, a better friend, well, maybe Sanford would still....

CHAPTER 24

Mid morning two days later.

TICK TICK HHHSSS TICK TICK HHHSSS.

The car's air conditioner ticked and wheezed; it was suffering asthma or emphysema, maybe even black lung like Ernie Norton. Traffic was backed up from the Cathedral at the top of Main Street hill all the way down past the Courthouse. No vehicle was moving. Everything under the scorching sun—cars, pedestrians, traffic cops, asphalt—everything seemed about to turn to taffy. Doc's starched shirt collar had rubbed raw a spot near his Adam's apple. He tugged at it with no good effect. He growled, "What a day for a funeral."

Heaving his weight onto one buttock, he gazed out the car's back window. He counted more than twenty cars back there, and he knew there were ten ahead of his in line inching toward the funeral home.

At a spot just beyond the crest of the hill and before the old railroad bridge stood *Hanrihan's Haven of Perpetual Rest*. It was originally the imposing, 3-story red brick mansion of dry goods merchant Noah Gunderman. Seamus Hanrihan had it painted white when he converted it. Its spot on Main Street hill had been an ideal location for Mr. Gunderman, it being only a five-minute downhill stroll to his emporium, but for the Sutersberg Police Department and for the town in general, Hanrihan's was a nuisance. Even a small cortege of mourners would cause traffic to back all the way down the hill, turning downtown Sutersberg into a hive of harassed hornets.

Now impatient and uncomfortable in the middle of the hornet's nest, Doc fumed, "What a goddamn mess."

Silence from Celia, who stared rigidly ahead. Occasionally she sniffed and touched a tissue to her nose; otherwise she might as well have turned to stone.

Doc looked out his side window. "Of all places for a funeral parlor. Why in hell would anyone want to use *Hanrihan's*?"

"How about, for a little dignity?" Celia replied, startling him. "You only get it once in this hick town, when you're dead. But a little dignity is nice to have for a change." Her voice had a quavering edge. "Besides, you've forgotten about the rituals. Mr. Hanrihan is the only mortician trained in the rituals. Whatever they are."

Lack of sleep had drawn dusky circles around Celia's eyes, making them look sunken. With that exception, she was showing a fairly normal face to the world. But the world was a stranger; Doc saw other things: her rigidity, for instance, as if her backbone were starched, and the way she had been abnormally submissive this morning. Half a dozen times Doc had reached over and patted her shoulder, expecting to be frowned at and shrugged off. He hadn't been. She was upset, for sure.

Doc said, "Oh, right. I'd forgotten about the rituals."

There had never been a Jewish mortician in Pizza County. Until a few years back, local people of the Jewish faith had to be transported to Pittsburgh to meet their maker. Then Seamus Hanrihan finally proved to the man who at that time was Rabbi of Sutersberg's Temple Adath Israel that he, a gentile, had been certified and could be trusted to care for Jewish corpses. Since then all Jewish funerals took place at *Hanrihan's Haven of Perpetual Rest.*

Seamus was a resourceful man, Doc knew. He said aloud, "Leave it to Seamus."

He waited in vain for a reply from Celia. She was shivering; Doc thought to open a window. Some impatient driver was fool enough to blow his horn, and others joined in.

Celia moaned, or was that the air conditioner? Her lower lip was extended and she was using her breath to cool her face.

Doc zipped up the window.

He tried to distract himself by watching the antics of one of Nuzzi's uniformed stooges, who waved his arms, repeatedly blew a whistle and otherwise managed to aggravate the drivers without improving the situation one bit.

Let sleeping dogs lie, damn fool, Doc thought. As he expected, the traffic light changed without any movement in the jam, and car horns began to bleat. The car immediately in front of his continued to bleat after the others had calmed down. Its driver leaned out of his window—who but Leo Drylie could get so much of himself out a car window?—and shook a fist at the cop. The line of traffic reacted to Leo's threats and curses by staggering forward three car lengths before stalling once again.

Resting his elbows on the steering wheel, Doc lifted his glasses and pinched the bridge of his nose.

He said, "Jeez, I feel rotten, all upside down and inside out. And exhausted. I'll bet I haven't slept in…"

WHAP! WHAP! Frustrated at the poor performance of the car's air conditioner, Celia karate chopped the top of the dashboard.

She said, "What's wrong with this damn thing?"

Once again he reached to pat her shoulder. This time, though, the gesture elicited the shrug-off he'd been expecting. What a relief. Doc hadn't realized it, but the closer they got to *Hanrihan's* the more not seeing that shrug-off had worried him. Now he knew that she was getting her act together. Under his breath, he muttered, "Atta girl."

She snapped at him, "Take a pill. I said, take a pill. If you can't sleep, take a pill."

"After what he did?" Doc nodded toward *Hanrihan's*, meaning Sanford. "No, thanks. Besides, I'm not supposed to, remember? Dr. Sam said not to." He squeezed his eyes tight shut. "What a nightmare. I mean, the heat's bad enough, but just look out there. The whole town's jamming into *Hanrihan's*. People that didn't even know Sandy."

The steering wheel felt cool against his forehead. "If only we didn't have to sit in this traffic."

Celia pointed her chin at the windshield. "Looks like you'll get your wish."

A young man built like the trunk of an oak tree, wearing a 3-piece black suit was moving down the line of cars. Each time he leaned in a driver's window to converse with a car's occupants, they would abandon the car in the street.

Was it bad breath, Doc wondered? *Or did the young man have bad news*? The farther along the line he moved, the deeper were the corrugations of concern on his forehead. Celia checked out the young man's suit coat as he attached funeral flags on their car.

It was possible to buy a decent suit in several places in Pizza County, but most Sutersberg men bought their clothing at *Parnelli & Slade Haberdashers*. Celia always insisted she could pick a Pizza County man out of a crowd by the poor cut of his suit.

The young man in the black suit by *Parnelli &
Slade* rapped on Doc's window.

Doc lowered it and said, "'lo, Willie."

Of course Doc knew Willie, Seamus Hanrihan's
second child and only son. Besides knowing just about
everyone in town, Doc was responsible for the bril-
liance of Willie's smile. As a member of the high
school varsity golf squad, one of his teammates had
altered Willie's smile with a pitching wedge. Acci-
dentally, he assured Doc while Doc was struggling
to restore Willie's maxillary anterior teeth.

"You folks goin' to the cemetery?" Willie asked,
an ear-to-ear grin with bubble gum stuck to Doc's
handiwork. Then he saw who he was talking to. "Hey,
looky here! How the hell are ya, Doc?"

Through the window came Willie's huge, meaty
paw; Doc, thinking his hands were precious, ignored
the gesture. He said, "I thought you were away at
school, Willie, but I guess you're working for your
dad now."

"Yeah, I graduated a couple weeks ago." Willie
stepped back a few paces to show off his suit. "How
do you like these threads, Doc? Old man Parnelli's
finest. And I'm certified, now, in F.A. & S."

"Come again?"

"That's Funerary Arts & Sciences." Willie poked
at the wad of gum with his tongue; Doc expected him
to blow a bubble.

Celia moaned. "Christ!"

"O say," Willie said, peering over at Doc's passenger. "Hiya, Mrs. G."

Celia stared stonily straight ahead, but Doc could see her lips begin to twist into a snarl. Doc jumped in with, "She's not feeling very sociable right now, Willie. Not at the moment."

"Off yer game today, eh, Mrs. G?"

Still acting as her mouthpiece, Doc said, "Mr. Klein was a good friend." The name didn't seem to ring a bell with Willie; Celia's breathing became a hiss. "You want us to leave the car here in the street, Willie?"

"Right, Doc, and leave the keys. I'll try to keep an eye on it for ya, but I got a helluva lot of cars to watch. This guy..." He tossed his thumb toward his father's funeral parlor. "He musta been popular. The whole town's turnin' out to see him under."

Celia dug her nails into the vinyl upholstery.

"Move it, Willie," Doc warned, shoving his door open. "And what you said about Mr. Klein? No, he wasn't popular. Nobody knew him, not even his best friend. You've been away at school too long to know, but Mr. Klein was The Invisible Man."

Willie swallowed his gum.

Doc continued to grumble as he walked around the car. When he offered Celia a hand out of the car, she surprised him by accepting it. She needed help, for sure: her knees looked totally unreliable, as if she could be played up and down like a yoyo. It reminded him of that day—how long ago?—when he'd brought Celia from Carnegie Tech to meet his parents. Now, as then, she appeared to be extremely vulnerable. She had applied very little makeup and in that cruel July daylight a flash from out of nowhere stunned Doc:

> *A black and white newsclip that he'd seen long ago of Katherine Hepburn being helped from a limo at Spencer Tracy's funeral: that gaunt face, those taut, colorless lips and darkly shadowed, haggard, fearful eyes.*

He thought she wouldn't like what the light was doing to her. "You okay, Ceilie?"

"Give me a minute, Jack, and I'll be fine." She dug a pair of dark-lensed RayBans from her purse and slipped them on. Immediately the mourning part of her face disappeared; the rest looked remarkably serene. Her entire body seemed to take strength, as if sensing that an advantage had been gained. She shrugged her shoulders, once, twice, straightened up to her full height and breathed deeply.

"Now, Jack," she announced, and stepped onstage. Tech-walked across the street and up the hill toward *Hanrihan's.*

She set the pace and Doc held her lightly by the elbow. They passed parked cars, utility poles, a fire hydrant, stepped down one curb and up another, avoided cracks in the walk, passed in and out of shady patches.

At the foot of *Hanrihan's* driveway, she signaled with a twitch of the elbow that she was ready to solo. He nodded and said, "Go, babe."

She turned to him and nodded. There were tiny furrows on her brow, but they disappeared almost immediately. He let her go ahead while he dropped back for a better view.

"Coming? Or are you just gonna stand there?" A hands-on-hips pose, impatient but not really angry. "I'll kill you if you stare at my ass."

"Hey, I'm just…"

"Oh, never mind. Come along. You'll be late for your own funeral."

CHAPTER 25

As a boy Seamus Hanrihan earned spending money by doing part-time summer chores for Noah Gunderman's gardener. He, along with several other boys, weeded flower beds, trimmed along the footpaths that traversed the estate, snipped unruly grass blades that sprouted up between flagstones and occasionally whitewashed the cobblestones that edged the carriageway. Doc knew this about Seamus because he and Seamus were in school together from grade school all the way through Pizza County High.

In the years between the Eisenhower and Kennedy administrations, Old Lady Gunderman's outdoor tea parties on sultry afternoons were famous among the swells of the County; invitations to those parties were prized. Or so young Seamus supposed as he watched wide-eyed dozens of black limousines and leather-upholstered convertibles cruise past him up that carriageway. The dry goods merchant and his twittering-bird of a wife would greet their guests beneath the white-pillared portico at the front of the house. Seamus, his brush dripping whitewash onto the grass, would gawk at the elegant personages who debarked from those shining, chrome-glittering cars: the men wearing linen trousers and jackets of Ivy League cut, the beautiful women with pageboy coifs and pleated skirts that showed a lot of knee.

Those days were for the Gundermans the good old days. Today, though Pizza County's only department store still bore his name, Noah Gunderman had squandered away the bulk of his fortune as well as the store. Also lost were his left leg to diabetes and his wits to dementia.

During the decade in which Seamus was growing from boyhood to manhood, the Gundermans continued to haunt their mansion on Main Street hill—he a gray, hobbling recluse and she a lonely old bird having tea alone. They died heirless and intestate within two years of each other during the Vietnam War years. Some local folks called it poetic justice. But less vindictive souls were willing to admit they had fantasized about chugging up that carriageway in a chauffeured limousine, or had wished they had been invited to sip Mrs. Gunderman's tea from a china cup with a pinkie pointed heavenward.

To most Sutersbergers it seemed a damn shame that the mansion had become *Hanrihan's Haven of Perpetual Rest*. However when tax liens had brought the house to auction, Seamus Hanrihan was the only interested party.

Time and neglect had ravaged the mansion; it and the surrounding property had gone to seed and weed.

Inside and out, it needed to be extensively repaired and preserved. Would that deter a mortician? Hardly, since repairing and preserving were his stock in trade.

Still, it was easy enough for Doc to imagine Noah Gunderman spinning in his grave when Seamus converted the wine cellar into an embalming room. And Mrs. Gunderman, what a turn she must've taken when Seamus began using her bedroom for casket selection.

The living, dining, and music rooms of the first floor, with their mahogany wainscoting and vast ceilings with baroque plasterwork, had been tailor-made for visitation suites; at least Seamus thought so. They needed only a bit of sprucing up. The same sprucing up was called for on the antebellum front portico. But the sight of Seamus Hanrihan standing beneath that portico attending the arrival of his guests brought down-in-the-mouth faces to people who remembered the Gundermans kindly.

"Speaking of the devil," Doc muttered, not realizing that he hadn't been speaking, but at that moment Seamus Hanrihan could be seen standing at his expected post beneath the portico.

Like his young son Willie, Seamus was a florid, beefy man; unlike Willie, who could be mistaken for a saloonkeeper, Seamus's posture, dress and manner epitomized the decorum of his profession. He exuded mortuary—sarcophagal, Doc thought—dignity. In Seamus's presence one was inclined to walk on tiptoes and converse in a whisper. Dressed in striped trousers, gray vest and cutaway coat, he set a very dignified, if bygone, tone.

When the Goldensons approached him, Seamus bowed from the waist and announced to no one in particular, "Doctor Goldenson."

Next he ogled Celia and with sweeping, open palms he announced her as if she were being presented to the Queen. He crooned, "And here be the lovely *Mrs.* Goldenson."

Like father, like son, Doc thought. He couldn't see Celia's eyes behind the dark glasses, but he could see the tight set of her jaw.

Celia stated, "*Mister* Hanrihan," and ducked past him into the foyer.

"Well, there, I've gone and done it, Doc, and I meant no harm." The mortician dried his palms on his trousers. "I'd heard that your missus…uh, I knew she'd be upset. I meant only to cheer her up."

The two men were teammates in the Elks Club Thursday Night Bowling League. Doc knew for a fact that Seamus had never been nearer to Ireland than the meetinghouse of the *Sons of the Shamrock Benevolent Association* on Pennsylvania Avenue. Still, his speech bore a touch of the peat bog whenever he was under pressure: when the team was counting on Seamus to bring in a difficult spare, or during a large funeral.

"I wanted to cheer her up, is all. I meant no harm, y' know."

"Never mind, Seamus," Doc said. "She's upset by Mr. Klein's death. We both are."

"You both are?" Seamus squeezed his right eye shut; he scrutinized Doc with the other one. Eventually he dismissed what he'd been thinking with a wave of the hand. "Of course, y' are. Of course." He excused himself and went off to greet other mourners.

He'd heard the rumors about Sandy and Celia, no doubt in Doc's mind about that. He trailed after Seamus, wanting to poke a finger in that scrutinizing eye of his. He caught the mortician by the sleeve of his coat and demanded, "I saw that snotty look, Seamus, and if you meant what I think you meant…"

"Hold yer harses," Seamus yelped, struggling out of Doc's grasp. "You'll wrinkle me coat. There's none like it in the County. And, see there." He pointed toward the foyer. "There's yer missus. Searchin' for you, she is, and lookin' none too pleased."

None too pleased? Doc could tell by the rigidity of the upper part of her whipcord body that Celia was more than none too pleased. She was pissed. "I'll see you later, Seamus," Doc said, trying for a threat in his voice. He scurried inside.

Celia dug her nails into his coat sleeve and began to drag him along the hallway. After just a few steps Seamus hailed them in a stage whisper. "Doc! Mrs. G! Hold yer harses. Migosh, where's me brains?" Reaching them, he drew Doc and Celia into a huddle out of earshot of the other mourners in the hallway.

"Johnny Grimes is waitin' for you. In Repose Room 5, he is. To confer, he said, very hush hush, very important that he confer with you before you go in…" He nodded toward Slumber Suite 1. "To Mr. Klein." He pointed the way to Repose Room 5 before hustling back to the portico.

Entering the Repose Room, Doc felt the same trepidation as if it, too, contained the corpse of a good friend. Not so Celia, he noticed as she pulled him through the door.

It was no larger than 15 feet by 25, a room occasionally used for an economy funeral, but alternately used for the storage of artificial ferns and folding chairs. On one such chair—a hard one, by the way he was perched on it—sat John Grimes. He leapt to his feet, looking glad to have company.

He said, "I wanted you both to know before going in to face that crowd." He nodded toward the door. "What a mob scene. Our friends and fellow Countians…" He shrugged and shook his head. "Anyhoo. I wanted to tell you about a little, ahem, accident that happened in my office today.

"The M.E.'s official report from Pittsburgh came by fax first thing this morning. I was readin' it and enjoyin' my first smoke of the day." He amazed Doc by pulling a General MacArthur-style corncob pipe from his pocket. "Yes, well, damn if I didn't—clumsy fool, me—spill ashes all over that report." A mock-weary shake of the head. "All over it, and damn if it didn't catch fire. Rotten luck, huh? I tried my darndest, but by the time I got the fire out the report was illegible." He looked at Celia, looked at Doc, and shrugged. "You won't mention it to anyone, will you? I wouldn't want the voters to know how clumsy I am."

Doc held his breath.

The D.A. went on, "I had to ask Coroner Columbo to fill out the death certificate without seeing the M.E.'s report. And, well, he did. He might've raised a ruckus except he was in a hurry. Seems he's takin' his family for two weeks to the Jersey shore, and he was anxious to be on the road. So he filled out the death certificate and signed it."

He paused to search their faces.

"So Klein's death is officially a coronary. A heart attack. As far as his family is concerned, as far as the life insurance company is concerned, and all of them..." Another nod to the door. "As far as all of them are concerned, that's just what it was, a heart attack." Grimes was having difficulty meeting Celia's eyes, but he gave Doc a weak smile.

"There may have been something healing in Klein that his clients sensed and needed, I'll give you that. I didn't see it, but if you say so, Celia... Maybe I'll get a chance to ask a few of those women what they saw in him, they're all here. One thing I do know, he made a passel of enemies of their exes and they're all here, too. To see Klein under. But you were right, Celia, when you said we have to see to the living.

They've been through enough. So it's official. Klein died of a coronary."

Doc had been unable to look at Grimes while he'd been talking, but now he swallowed the lump in his throat and said, "Thanks...thanks an awful lot, Johnny."

Celia removed her dark glasses and touched her lips to Grimes's cheek. She replaced the glasses and without a word pulled Doc out of the room. In the hall she whispered, "Did you ever know John Grimes to smoke?"

"Once, in his old man's barn when we were kids."

She looked pleased. "Just as well. His face is too round, he'd look stupid smoking a pipe."

She stopped at the entrance to Slumber Suite 1. The rumble that could be heard through the door made it clear the place was filled beyond capacity.

She said, "Listen, that little *accident* of John's changed nothing as far as we're concerned; our job is the same. To tidy things up. We do want things tidied up, don't we, Jack?" Doc liked nothing better than having things tidy. He nodded. Celia said, "Good. All we've got to do is squelch the rumors about Sanford and me. To do that, we simply must put on a little theatrical in...there." She nodded at the door to Slumber Suite 1. "So." She faced the door and drew a full breath.

"So?"

It was an impatient breath that she exhaled. "So, while you're being the heartbroken friend, you've gotta be the very loving, very attentive husband at the same time. And while I'm consoling my dear friend, Millie, I'll play the demure, dependent, clinging-vine wife."

"I believe I am a very loving, attentive husband," Doc said, with certainty. Then, "Aren't I?"

"You certainly are, Jack. Yes, indeed." She patted his hand. "So I'm not asking for anything unusual, am I? Only, exaggerate a bit, okay? Play to the people in the last row, if you know what I mean."

Doc made a face but nodded.

Celia kissed him on the cheek as she had kissed Grimes a moment before. She whispered, "Don't take a shine to the clinging-vine wife. She'll be gone right after the funeral."

CHAPTER 26

Before actually entering one of Seamus Hanrihan's slumber suites, a mourner had first to pass through an anteroom. These were large rectangular rooms, carpeted and chandeliered but without furniture, to encourage people to stand in conversational groups and talk, as if they were at a cocktail party.

Seamus approached Death on reluctant tiptoes, not without respect and dignity but with a touch of humor. That being the case, Seamus had what he thought was a good reason for providing his slumber suites with anterooms: while visiting a patient in a hospital, people were in the habit of gathering in the corridors outside the sickroom and disturbing the patients with loud talk.

Visitors to funeral parlors did the same thing. They tried to distract each other from the funereal gloom with inane chatter about sports, politics and the weather—motivated by the fear of catching one's death.

To put some distance between this kind of small talk and the deceased, Seamus provided anterooms.

Doc and Celia made their entrance into the anteroom of Slumber Suite 1 clinging to each other as a loving couple should at a time of mourning, with somber eyes and mouths turned dejectedly down. Expecting the anteroom to be jammed with mourners, they were startled to find it empty.

The sounds of loud chatter and movement were coming from the slumber room, the door between it and the anteroom being slightly ajar. Doc looked at Celia; her left eyebrow was up. She had come to expect nothing good from Sutersbergers, and she realized, as her husband did, that the empty anteroom and the noise leaking from beyond the open door meant trouble. They knew, too, that it was out of their hands, whatever it was. They shrugged and approached the door. As Doc reached for the knob, the door flew toward him. At the head of a ripple of whispers, young Rabbi Mark Kaye blew through the open door, slammed it shut and leaned against it.

The Rabbi's youthful face was damp with perspiration. His wilting attempt at a beard was failing miserably, his puppy-brown eyes were goggled, concern had wrinkled his forehead and his blond brows were drawn into a single line. His *yarmulke* had escaped its bobby pin only to dangle precariously from one ear. He looked as if he'd just managed to escape the clutches of a wild beast, something they'd not prepared him for at the *Yeshivah*.

"Good grief," he said, resting his head against

the door while mopping his brow with a hankie. "Good grief."

When Mark Kaye was hired by the board of directors of Sutersberg's Temple Adath Israel two years ago, he was the youngest rabbi Doc had ever seen, and it was dislike at first sight.

Was it Kaye's youth that rankled? Or the rebuke in his New York-accented voice when he remarked on Doc's sporadic Temple attendance? Or his casually inappropriate manner of dress?

Like now, Doc thought, looking down his nose at Kaye's rumpled blue shirt, shapeless khaki trousers and faded dungaree jacket. Even his name wrankled Doc, who believed if a man's name is really Kwalwasser, he ought to call himself Kwalwasser, not Kaye.

The Rabbi's eyes lost some of their panic when he recognized the Goldensons. "D-doc," he gushed in relief. "Mrs. Goldenson. Thank…uh, thank God you're here."

It was not Rabbi Kaye's habit to acknowledge the existence of God; it was the first time Doc had heard him mention Him. He latched onto Doc's hand, shook it and blotted his palm on his khaki slacks before offering it to Celia. He said, "You've got to do something. They won't be controlled, I can't officiate."

"Who can't be controlled? What are you raving about?"

"It's not my fault. I went to comfort Mrs. Klein,

but she was, she's... But never mind, she's the least of it."

Doc pressed his ear to the door but could hear nothing through it, so he pulled the door slightly open and set his eye to the opening. As soon as it was opened, the chatter and cross talk of the *mourners* sounded to Doc as if he had his ear to a seashell. Doc likened the scene taking place in the slumber suite to what he might see at a wedding, with the bride's family and guests all seated on one side of the aisle and the groom's people all occupying the other side: here he saw a mostly female side, Sandy's clients, the ex wives—saddened, some of them making good use of their hankies—and a mostly male side—greeting each other cheerfully, high-fiving—the ex husbands.

On the male side in a pew near the door, Wally DelPaine was leaning far across the aisle to whisper something to the former Mrs. DelPaine, seated on the other side.

"Jeez," Doc muttered under his breath, "I didn't know they were on speaking terms."

Behind Wally DelPaine and behind Mrs. DelPaine, were seated the Espositos, the coach of the high school football team and his estranged wife, him laughing, she drying her eyes, both of them looking capable of taking positions on the Steelers offensive line. And behind them Knucky DeVito, the Goldensons' mailman, was yelling something across the aisle at his wife, who he had deserted the previous year. Knucky's present lover, who was sitting beside him, was being left out of the melee between husband and wife, and she looked as if that was okay with her. Doc couldn't remember her name but he remembered her nickname, *First Class*, given her by her fellow employees at the post office. Doc couldn't believe his eyes. There were Bert and Lowanda Burke, across the aisle from each other but at least in the same room for the first time in three, maybe four years.

"What's going on," Doc asked Rabbi Kaye. "Did the Messiah come?" He re-closed the door.

Rabbi Kaye was asking Celia, "What's his name, the little Napoleon with the deep voice?"

"Drylie?"

"That's him, Drylie. He walked right up to the closed casket... Walked, nothing. He marched like a toy soldier and demanded. You hear? Demanded!" Kaye was out of breath. " 'Lemme see the body,' he demanded. 'Lemme see it. I ain't leavin' till I see it.' "

"Can you imagine?" the Rabbi asked.

Yes, Celia could.

He said, "Well, I refused, of course. It's not customary with Jews, I said. But Drylie... He's not Jewish, is he?"

Doc reassured the Rabbi, whose eyes rolled gratefully heavenward, that Drylie was definitely not Jewish.

"I tried to explain about closed caskets. Why did

I even bother? Just wasted my breath. That, that Drylie didn't give a damn, he kept insisting on seeing the body. If I hadn't stiff-armed him…" The Rabbi made a move he'd undoubtedly seen on *Monday Night Football*. "…he would have pried open the lid. Sure as, as…hell, he would've." Out of breath again, Kaye sagged against the door.

Doc slammed a fist into his palm and cursed, "Damn that little bastard!"

"And Mrs. Klein," the Rabbi added. "Well, frankly, she's drunk. She's nipping from a bottle she's got in a brown paper bag."

"Oh no, Mil," Celia groaned. Doc was pummeling his palm as if it were Drylie's ugly mug. Celia managed to interrupt him. "We've got to get in there right now." She meant all of them, including the Rabbi, who didn't want to be included. "We have to get that bottle away from her."

"Oh no," the Rabbi said, "Don't think for a minute…not on your…"

"That's what you think," Doc interrupted. "If Celia says we have to go in, we go in, all of us including you. But not without Seamus. Somebody go get Seamus."

Obviously someone had already gone for Seamus because at that moment he burst into the anteroom. Responding to a warning of possible disorder in one of his slumber suites, Seamus's face and the determination in his stride were identical to what Doc saw on bowling nights as Seamus, attempting to convert a difficult spare, would approach the foul line: his bulldog face was a mask of determination, his brow was deeply furrowed and his tongue peeked out from the corner of his mouth.

Doc moved aside to allow Seamus a peek into Slumber Suite 1. He saw disrespect for the dead at least on the male side of the aisle.

"Jaysus, Mary and Joseph! Such carrying on in my Haven!" The indignation that swelled Seamus's chest seemed to lift him off the floor. He tugged his vest, took another moment as the look on his face hardened from bulldog to bull mastiff. Then he threw open the door and sallied forth into the suite.

Celia clutched the Rabbi's denim jacket and with precise diction that emphasized biting consonants and flashing dentals, she barked orders in his face.

"Just this once try to muster a little dignity. Not wisdom, I'm not asking for the impossible, just a little dignity. You could save the day, you know. It would be quite a feather in your cap if only you could…" She gave him a shake with each word. "See this through with dignity." She let go of the jacket, patted the wrinkles from it. "Jack and I will do the best we can, but really it's up to you and Mr. Hanrihan."

Then she spun him around and propelled him through the door.

Chapter 27

Amoment later Celia, pale and demure, came through the door on Doc's arm. They started up the center aisle. Along with the scraping sounds of shuffling feet, tittering from the male side and snuffling in hankies from the distaff side, their progress was accompanied by a rippling murmur of gossip that grew louder with their every step. Doc imagined himself crossing the Red Sea in between roiling walls of water.

Suddenly he was stopped. Somehow he had managed to snag the sleeve of his suit coat on…

Leo Drylie's tiny, hairy-knuckled hand gripped Doc's coattail. In a stage-whisper of a basso that everyone in the chapel could hear, Drylie said, "We been waitin' for ya, Doc. We ain't used to seein' the Invisible Man without his sidekick." Drylie turned to his neighbors, seeking their approval. His legs swung back and forth under the pew without reaching the floor.

"No point in goin' up there," he said to Doc, nodding toward the front of the room. "The laughs are back here."

Melvina Toth was seated on the side with Sanford's clients. Being unmarried and on Public Assistance, Melvina had no dealings with Sanford; Melvina was the albatross hanging from Doc's neck. She grinned at him and tapped her denture-less lower gum.

Seated next to Melvina wearing a gray tweed business suit that smelled of mothballs was Drylie's sharp-featured bitch of an ex-wife, Amelia. She had lost weight since he'd seen her last. Her face, thin before, now looked hatchet sharp.

Doc didn't dare say that, or anything else, to Amelia.

Leo tugged on Doc's sleeve. "The widow's got herself a snoot fulla booze and the Invisible Man's really dead. Believe me, I checked to make sure."

Acid reflux burned Doc's throat; he gulped air in an attempt to relieve it and hurried after Celia. While he'd been occupied by the Drylies, Doc had lost track of Celia. She was nowhere in sight. Doc assumed she'd gone directly into the cubicle adjacent to the casket platform reserved for the bereaved family. She meant to take Millie in hand, no doubt.

Seamus Hanrihan, looking angry enough to bite, stood in front of the casket with his arms folded across his chest. The room full of mourners had been frozen into relative silence by his icy glare. He kept the glare pointed at them as if he were holding them at gunpoint. The Rabbi could be seen hiding unsuccessfully behind a potted fern. The silence in the room felt tenuous, as if an overblown balloon were at any moment threatening to burst.

As Doc approached the casket, Seamus relinquished his position in front and moved around behind it. Doc was close enough now to touch the casket, but he couldn't bring himself to do so. He could only stare at it and try to lose himself in the swirls of its dark walnut grain. He had things to say to his best friend, but there was no privacy here; he felt the eyes of the crowd on his back. He sought comfort in one of the darker compartments of his mind. He gained entrance, but not easily because the lump behind his ear began to throb—he cursed Poke Perkins.

It wasn't working, first because there was no privacy but also because a mental compartment could not be found with shadows deep enough to conceal himself and, too, the throbbing ache from behind his ear now radiated down the back of his neck to the shoulder blade.

If only he could crawl off somewhere, some really dark, quiet place where he could be alone to mourn. He needed to embrace Sandy's death, fold it carefully and tuck it away inside himself. To feel its emptiness, be hurt by it, cry over it and hopefully be cleansed by the tears. But there hadn't been time; still wasn't. The idea seemed luxurious at the moment. He came out of the darkness to find his eyes still following the grain in the walnut wood. He thought, Some other time, old friend.

While Doc had been lost in thought, Rabbi Kaye had finally abandoned his refuge behind the potted fern. Just as Doc looked up, Kaye proceeded to the lectern that had been placed to the left of the casket. He shrugged at Seamus, which the mortician took as a signal to open the door to the family cubicle.

Now visible to the mourners in the chapel were Millie and little Ellie, dressed inappropriately in a pink pinafore and black patent leather shoes; Celia was seated between them with an arm wrapped protectively around each one.

At the moment the door had opened, Millie had been facing toward Doc; after that moment she kept her eyes down. Celia's idea, he was sure. But in that one moment when Millie faced him, she was an open book: she was snozzled with sherry and hollowed out by fatigue and grief. But more than that, she seemed to have reverted to childhood. She looked every bit as much a child as little Ellie, who looked as if she would've liked to put her thumb in her mouth, but dared not.

At a nod from Celia, Doc scuttled to take the empty seat next to the child. Ellie looked up at Doc and stuck her tongue out at him.

The Rabbi looked longingly at the potted fern; realizing that it wasn't to be, he looked as if about to suck *his* thumb. He began leafing through a thin blue book—slowly at first, then desperately when he seemed unable to find his place or his notes. He gave up and recited haltingly from memory a few phrases in Sephardic Hebrew, as Hebrew is spoken in Israel. To Doc, whose boyhood training had been in the Ashkenazic traditions of Central and Eastern Europe, the sound of it grated on his ears.

Rabbi Kaye leaned close to the microphone and said, "Psalm 8: Wh-what is man, O—WOO WOO WOO!" He leaned too close to the microphone and received a wailing rebuke. He backed off. "Or…or the s-son of man that Thou…uh, regardest him?" He looked genuinely surprised to have remembered that much. He slid back into Hebrew, then returned to English.

More confident now. "Man is like a breath; his days are shadows that pass away." The rest of the psalm eluded him. Were those last words from a different one? Who knew?

Kaye looked around at Seamus, hoping for a hint but getting an icy stare instead. He shrugged. "The essence of life, as if I knew what it… I mean, what we're all really uh, after all is said and…"

He was failing. He was in a position to get this crowd under control, and he was failing. What had happened to his notes? He searched for them again in the book and on the floor under the lectern, without success. He shrugged.

"I…uh, I haven't been sleeping at all well lately. The missus, my Esther, is as they say in the… somewhere in the Torah or…somewhere, my Esther is great with child. Yes she is, and she rolls around and grunts in her sleep and I can't…"

Seamus disapproved with a loud harrumph.

Kaye pleaded to Seamus. "I can't find it. I had a really cool segue from the word *shadow* in the Psalm to, you know, him." He pointed the book at the casket. "Mr. Klein. The Invisible Man."

A murmur ran through the crowd. Now they were listening.

"Anyhow, I fall immediately to sleep but next thing you know I'm wide awake an hour later. So I get out of bed and turn on the TV. I've been watching the late late show, mostly a lot of old movies, black and white ones even."

Kaye nodded. "S-so. One oldie in particular that I'm reminded of now is *The Shadow*, starring some old guy, Victor somebody. In the movie a guy that calls himself The Shadow could cloud men's minds so they couldn't see him. In other words, he could make himself invisible." Kaye made a face, "I know you get it, the guy in the movie can make himself invisible, kind of like Mr. Klein? But the thing is, even though the bad guys couldn't see The Shadow, they could still hear him, and if the bad guys had guns, which they usually did, they could shoot at the sound of his voice. So it was still awfully dangerous for the Shadow even though he was invisible.

"Did you know, you can get killed being invisible? Why, try crossing Main Street at rush hour if you think you'd like being invisible. You could, you could get killed being invisible.

"The thing I'm driving at is this: an invisible man is still there. Even though he can't be seen, he's still actually there. He can still be hurt. If we think about it, if we're honest with ourselves, we, all of us, had a good laugh at Mr. Klein's expense. For fun we called him The Invisible Man. We were unkind, too, we gossiped about him. We did, we…I remember something from my studies at the *Yeshiva*, something about gossip being the Devil's tool, uh, but that's from the other, the New Testament. But still, don't you think it's about time we cut him some slack?

"Somebody, an ancient rabbi…I think, once said, 'L-let…uh, let him who bears no guilt cast the first stone.' Okay? Okay."

Kaye peered at Seamus, searching the mortician's face for a sign of approval. He shrugged.

Had Kaye just quoted Jesus Christ? Doc doubted it was appropriate, but he wasn't surprised.

CHAPTER 28

BLAAH BLAAH! SKREE! WHA WHA!

Stuck in traffic again; moving, only inching along but at least moving.

The Jewish cemetery was located beyond Suters-berg's partially-rural, partially-industrial south side, near the newly built public high school. Nearby, waist-high corn stalks in farmers' fields could be seen shouldering up against scruffy, rusted, abandoned buildings on deserted industrial lots. Since *Hanrihan's Haven* was on the northern edge of town and the cemetery was beyond the southern edge, the funeral cortege had to drag along the entire length of Main Street. Horns blared, crosstown traffic backed up and pedestrians gawked. Nuzzi's black-and-white vehicle, siren wailing and roof bar winking red and blue, led the way through a gauntlet of eyes. Merchants and customers alike abandoned the Main Street shops to gather at curbside to count the cars following the hearse.

It had always been the custom in Pizza County to count the number of cars in funeral processions. Long after the actual funeral had been forgotten— and most of the essence of the deceased had been forgotten as well—a Countian might recall: "Hell yes, I remember old Stuffy Galligher. He got one helluva sendoff. Twenty-two cars." Or they would roll their eyes upward and quickly finger a cross on the air over their chests. "Rafe Weingarten? I remember Rafe, alright. Skinflint bastard got what he deserved, only a five-car."

Doc recalled that as a youngster he had asked his father to explain why folks counted the cars.

"Now there's a question. Why?" As he pondered, Earl Goldenson combed his fine gray hair with his fingers. "It has to do with friends, Doc, with how many friends you've got. It's not easy to tell, you know, not when you're alive. When you're dead, it's easy—just count the cars." How could you count the cars if you're dead? That changed the elder Goldenson's combing to scratching. "Now there's a question, huh, sonny? There's a question."

As the cortege crept slowly down Main Street, Doc imagined his father at the curb in front of his fur salon; Earl looked very surprised. His lips moved silently as he scratched his head and counted the cars. By the old man's car-counting theory, Sandy rivaled in popularity the former Bishop of the Pizza County Catholic Diocese, His Holiness Antonio Piazza, after whom the County was named and whose funeral in 1949 had been a legendary 112-car.

A uniformed cop was stationed at every intersection, including people Doc had never seen in uniform;

undoubtedly they were the part-timers Nuzzi called his *hourlies*. He had never seen as many officers employed for a funeral. Leave it to Nuzzi to turn a funeral into a spectacle.

Doc's car was approaching the corner of Fourth & Main, where one of the hourlies stood in some semblance of parade rest.

Another man, pear-shaped like his boss, who had trouble keeping his pants up. When he raised his arms to restrain traffic, Doc could see huge sweat stains.

Doc wondered what kind of shape his teeth were in. He'd never seen pear-shaped teeth, but…"

"Damnit, Jack." Celia's voice snapped him out of his reverie. "You didn't hear a word I said."

"Ummm, sorry. I was daydreaming, thinking about…things. Traffic jams, fat cops."

"And fish in glass bowls." Celia nodded toward the curb. "Feel those eyes."

She was curled up on the seat with her back to the window and her legs tucked under her skirt. She giggled. "I feel like a goldfish. Celia Goldfish."

The cortege picked up speed at the foot of the hill. Doc would have preferred keeping an eye on Celia—she sounded on the edge of hysteria—but he had to watch the road.

"They were counting cars, weren't they?" Rhetorical.

"It's nothing, Ceilie, just a habit they have. They don't mean anything by it."

"Oh, I know, I know."

Doc recognized her peevish tone; without looking he knew her jaw was jutting out.

"You can't blame Sutersbergers. I learned that a long time ago. You can't blame them for anything. No sir and no ma'am, they mean no harm. You know, Jack, you say that a lot? You do. You say, they mean no harm a lot. Well, dammit, but…maybe not, but God! The small minds. God save me from the small minds."

"Jeez, you must be exhausted. Sure you're all right?"

"Huh. I feel…loopy. One minute I'm light-headed, the next I feel used up, drained." She removed the dark glasses and rubbed her eyes. "It's a good thing the service wasn't any longer. I'm exhausted. Between putting on a good show and, well, with Mil and Ellie leaning on me for support, I'm done in. When we left Hanrihan's, I thought there wasn't a drop of energy left in me, not in my whole body. I thought I would crash right there in Seamus's carriageway."

Touch her hair, rub the back of her neck, do something, anything. He wanted to badly, but he was driving.

She patted his arm. "I'll be all right, Jack, really." A moment's pause. "Actually, I feel better than I expected to. Things went pretty well, considering. I think the Rabbi's sermon, if you could call it that, did a lot of good, don't you? Calmed things down a bit?"

Doc shrugged.

"You don't think so? I do. I feel lighter, less weighted down."

Another pause.

"I didn't know Mark Kaye had it in him. Hmm. '*We may not have been able to see him but he was there. An invisible man can be hurt.*' I didn't know he had it in him."

"Maybe you ought to shake him more often."

The hearse made a slow turn through a wrought-iron gate and gained the cemetery grounds.

"Oh." Was it that Celia hadn't anticipated the change in speed? She clutched at her chest.

It was nothing, really, only a cemetery; a nice one as cemeteries went. They entered to face a grassy expanse of hillside, a gradual climb, with brass plates inlaid into the grassy turf to mark the gravesites—the new section. To the far right was the old section, beginning at the foot of the hillside and stretching for maybe thirty or forty yards, a field of tightly-packed, chaotically-placed gravestones looking like crooked teeth. Halfway up the hill of the new section, beside the narrow asphalt ribbon of road that led up to it, a green carpet of artificial grass and a green tent had been pitched over the gravesite to shade the mourners from the relentless sun.

Beside the tent on the right was a pile of clay, shale and dirt covered discretely with another green carpet. On the left side a huge, dreadful yellow praying mantis—a backhoe, frozen in place, waiting, as patient as Fate. Celia grabbed Doc's hand. He wanted to say something comforting, but words jammed in his throat.

The cortege seemed to hesitate at the gate, as if rolling onto sacred ground would disturb the slumber of those within. But the hearse had no such trepidations; it made its plodding advance up the asphalt path and pulled up beside the tent. The cortege took courage with a tremor and a sigh, and followed.

No one moved out of his car; no noise. Nothing to disturb…anyone.

It was not a place Doc would ordinarily choose to pull off the road on a bright summer day, but it was a serene, green place. And what a view! Sandy would be able to see the entire southern half of the valley from there. Along the edges of the cemetery a line of pin oaks and red maples bordered the manicured grounds. Off to the right, rooftops: Sutersberg and the Courthouse dome were visible. Straight ahead beyond the highway, more hills, more trees, more rooftops: the Oak Hill Plan. Off to the left, farms. Doc could see fuzzy yellow tops of waist-high corn stalks. Beyond the farms, more rooftops: Doc realized it was the campus of the Community College. Sandy would like having a college campus in sight.

Not a hint of a breeze, but Doc dismissed the urge to loosen his tie and collar. Once again his eyes drifted along the length of the valley: no movement on the highway, no movement in the air; Doc thought the world was waiting, but for what?

Then Willie Hanrihan's head protruded from the driver's window of the hearse. His brow showed deep concern as he peered at the black limo that contained his father, Millie and little Ellie. The limo's darkly tinted glass prevented the intrusion of prying eyes. Doc, too, was equally concerned at the delay.

Willie left the hearse, the sound of his door slamming echoed to the right and down the hillside to rebound off the gravestones of the old section. Willie swaggered to the limo, and once a rear passenger window had rolled down, Willie stuck his head inside. Earlier in this seemingly endless day, Doc remembered, passengers had abandoned their cars when Willie stuck his head inside. Doc—Willie's dentist—was still worried about Willie's breath.

Willie made way for the opening of the limo door; Seamus stepped out and took Ellie's hand. His lips moved rapidly, his head bobbed occasionally and the hand not holding Ellie reached into the limo. It came out empty. Seamus turned a desperate look toward the Goldenson car.

Celia said, "Damn," sounding guilty. "I was afraid of this. Millie won't get out. I knew I should have stayed with her."

"Seamus said he could handle her. You believed him."

"Huh. I wanted to believe him, but I really didn't. Well here I go." She slammed the door. "Damn damn damn!"

Doc would have liked to follow her only with his eyes, but reluctantly he stepped out of the car.

Other people took that as a signal and exited their cars, too—just as reluctantly. To stand beside their cars was as far as anyone seemed willing to go.

Celia's I-mean-business stride got her to the limo quickly. Willie and Seamus saw her coming and cleared out of the way. She continued to mean business as, with hands on hips, she peered into the limo.

She didn't say anything, at least Doc didn't see her lips move. Even if she had, he was too far away to hear. No matter. He'd heard often enough the tone that went with his wife's I-mean-business posture.

Millie came out of the limo—fast. Doc wagged his head, *Wouldn't you know it*? With Millie on his arm, little Ellie in hand and Celia following, Seamus Hanrihan led the way to the hearse. Willie greeted their arrival by throwing open the rear doors. There, waiting patiently, was the walnut casket.

Doc kicked one of his tires. Willie, sounding perturbed, called to the mourners, "Hey, yu'ns with the gloves? Step on it, will ya."

Seamus, face drained, growled at him. Willie gaped at his father. He said, "Oh, yeah." He waved a gray glove over his head. The signal.

Doc had hoped it would never come. His left knee jerked spasmodically, but he couldn't hang back any longer. He reached into the car for the gray gloves Seamus had given each pall bearer. He stepped up to join the other five men at the rear of the hearse. As he did so Little Ellie reached to take hold of him but Seamus intervened by refusing to let go of her. She stuck out her tongue at him.

The pallbearers took the positions assigned by Seamus, three on each side of the casket: at one end, the two tallest men, Doc and John Grimes; in the middle, Victor Shumacher—thin and dour-faced like his sister Helga, Sandy's secretary—and Herb Fowler, president of the *First National Bank* that held the mortgage to the Klein home. At the other end, two very short men, the Honorable Sotirios Petropoulis, President Judge of Piazza County Court of Common Pleas—his head large and hairless as a ping pong ball—and across from him Andy Porko, Sandy's barber.

They took hold of the brass handles and heaved. The weight shifted precariously, the casket tilting severely toward the two short men. Doc gave Seamus a doubtful look, which Seamus answered with a wink. Sure enough, when they began to climb the knoll toward the tent, with the judge and the barber leading the way, the casket began to level off; the steeper the hill became, the more level the casket. Sandy wouldn't spill out. Doc sighed and nodded to Seamus.

The bearers overcame their initial faltering and swung into a grunting cadence—uht hum, uht hum, uht hum—rather like a heartbeat. Concentrating on the rhythm nearly hypnotized Doc—uht hum, uht hum, uht hum—lulled him into a trance.

Rabbi Kaye, who had been hanging back, stumbled past and took his position in front of the casket. Doc hardly noticed him. The incongruous sight of Kaye marching before the coffin, imprecating the Angel of Death with an ancient droning chant might have given Doc a chuckle. Had he not been in a trance.

The bearers placed the casket on nylon lowering straps that suspended it over the grave; then they removed their gloves, set them gingerly on the coffin lid and dispersed into the crowd.

Doc stood alone with his gloves in hand, unable to bring himself to discard them. Instead he waited. Listening intently—for what?

He didn't know why it felt possible, but it did: if he waited, Sandy might have a parting word. Besides, why not keep the gloves? He liked them. They fit well. Come wintertime, they'd look smart with his charcoal topcoat.

But Sandy had nothing to say. Except for Millie's sniffling, the Rabbi's throat-clearing, a lot of feet-shuffling and from the general direction of the backhoe, Ernie Norton's tortured breathing—except for these, there was silence.

A chilling thought pinched its way into Doc's trance, a bit of lyric from his and Sandy's favorite Civil War ballad:

> *Something's breathing in the silence,*
>
> *Only Death makes such a sound.*

It shook him out of his trance.

He mumbled, "Shit. Goodbye, Sandy." He surrendered the gloves and went to stand with the women.

CHAPTER 29

Rabbi Kaye tried to hand Doc a pamphlet with the words of the *Kaddish* printed on it, but Doc knew the prayer by heart so he didn't need it. Kaye persisted.

He said, "Here, help the Kleins." Then to the gathering, "Let's all of us, uh, those who are able, recite the *Kaddish*, the Hebrew prayer of mourning." He nodded at Doc, pulled in his neck and hid his eyes behind his hymnal.

"*Yitkadal v'yitkadash...*" In the stillness his hesitant voice sank leaden to the tent's Astroturf carpeting.

Doc picked it up: "*Sh'may rabbah, amen.*" He held the pamphlet for Millie. Although she was mumbling incoherently, Doc noticed Millie's eyes were closed.

He stooped to hold the pamphlet for Ellie, following the words alliterated in English with his index finger, but then he didn't know if an eight year old could handle alliterated Hebrew. The words were tongue-twisters even for adults, let alone a child.

Ellie did the best she could, sighed from the effort at the conclusion and warmed Doc with a smile. He allowed his mind to wander:

Before Grandpa Goldenson's funeral—Doc was twelve at the time—he had rehearsed the *Kaddish*, reading the words over and over until they were memorized. Seemed silly now. Doc couldn't remember what childish notion had made it urgent to have the *Kaddish* memorized. Maybe stumbling on the words would cause trouble in Heaven for Grandpa Goldenson? He grinned at the memory of himself—crazy kid—rehearsing the *Kaddish* until he could mumble it like the bearded old men at the synagogue. A talent of doubtful value. Still, it had come in handy—hadn't it?—at the many funerals he had attended lately. How many? Jeez. Two contemporaries of his parents, one of his dental patients and one of his high school chums. He felt dizzy; he feared he might drop the pamphlet. Cancer, heart attacks and a stroke at age fifty. He'd seen them off…to wherever, dispatched them with a mindless drone of the *Kaddish*.

He was surrounded by the women and the child, but he felt overwhelmed by loneliness. The words of the *Kaddish* turned scarlet, seared his throat with acid. Unable to read the pamphlet, he blinked his eyes rapidly. Dad. Mom. Sandy!

"*V'yimru amen*." Rabbi Kaye followed the Hebrew words with a psalm in English.

By the end of it, Doc had dried his eyes and eased the heartburn with several deep breaths. At that moment Kaye, searching for something around the grave, began to slip into panic mode again. He gaped at

Seamus, who glared at Willie. Eventually a light went on in Willie's head that lit up his face.

He said, "Oh, yeah." He exited the tent and returned carrying a cardboard box of dirt. After placing the box beside the grave, Willie looked to his father for approval. He got a grimace.

The Rabbi reached into the box for a handful of dirt, held it up for all to see. "From the dust of the earth did He take us up." He followed that with, "Uh, and to the dust He returns us." His eyebrows went up as if the very idea startled him. Doc expected Kaye to say, Jeez! but he didn't. Instead it appeared as if he were touched by divine inspiration. It was all over his face when he looked up from his hymnal.

"If we can praise God for creating life, maybe we shouldn't hold it against Him for taking it back." That said, he sent the dirt skittering onto the casket lid.

Seamus approached Doc, Millie, Ellie and Celia, who were all huddled together. He said, "It's customary for members of the family to sprinkle some dirt." He nodded at the casket. Doc noticed that Seamus's brogue had disappeared. "It signifies a bending to God's will. A primitive custom but...not the child, of course, unless..." Seamus shrugged. "Or if you'd rather not..."

Without hesitation Millie stepped forward. Doc admired her fortitude, even though she approached the box as if it contained dynamite instead of dirt. Unfortunately someone—most likely Willie—chose that moment to activate the mechanism that lowered the casket. Millie recoiled as the casket began to slowly sink into the ground. With a yelp she pegged a handful of dirt at the lid as it disappeared below the Astroturf. She returned to the huddle, flushed and breathless.

"How'd I do?" she asked. Celia patted her hand.

"Hey, nice throw, Mrs. K," Willie called.

Celia had an odd—for her—look on her face, as if she were surprised by her own desire. She said, "I think I want to…you know." She pointed her chin at the grave. "That is, if you don't mind, Mil?"

Millie didn't mind. Doc thought Celia might stumble, the way she dragged her feet on the Astroturf. Celia held a handful of dirt over the grave for several seconds before finally opening her fingers and allowing the dirt to simply spill out. Doc gaped at her. She was smiling and her movements seemed lighter when she returned to Millie's side.

"Poor Doc," Millie teased him with a crooning, pouty mouth. "You look so tired. Was Sandy awfully heavy?" She tittered like a child, wide-eyed, and clapped a hand over her mouth. No use. More tittering leaked past her lips and between her fingers. She hissed—almost lip-farted—and her body quivered.

Damn that sherry, Doc thought, but what Millie said struck him close to the bone. His guilt had the weight of a huge boulder. If he bent over and applied all of his strength, he might manage to hoist it off the ground as far as his knees and no further. He hadn't the strength or the will to raise it higher than that, nor could he put it down. He could tell, he would never be able to put it down.

He took both women by an arm and began leading them away when Ellie tugged his pant leg. She wanted to take her turn with the dirt. This child held no end of surprises for Doc, but he obliged and held the box while she took a tiny handful, and he held her around the waist as she stretched way out over the open grave and let the dirt go.

Doc said, "Good job, sweetheart. C'mon now, we're all done here."

They had barely stepped off the Astroturf when— RATTLE RATTLE PING. And again—RATTLE RATTLE. A third time. Volley after volley struck the casket.

Doc turned to see a crowd, not Ernie Norton, who was leaning against the backhoe gasping for breath, but a half dozen of the ex husbands were gathered around the open grave.

He couldn't actually see what they were doing, but the rattle of dirt against walnut was unmistakable. The Rabbi stumbled around the periphery of the crowd trying to establish order; Seamus hurried to assist him. Doc would have done the same if Celia and Millie, holding him by the arms, hadn't prevented it.

"Forget it, Jack," Celia said. "Why bother? Sanford is beyond needing your help. Or anybody else's."

After doing their bit with the dirt, each ex-husband walked away clapping dust from his hands and smiling; some even had their ex-wives in tow. Taking into account what he had seen at *Hanrihan's* and now at the cemetery, it seemed to Doc that Sandy's death brought some modicum of peace to a lot of formerly estranged people.

RATTLE RATTLE.

"Jeez," he said and turned his back on them.

Millie said, "Leave them be, Doc. They can't hurt him now; nobody can. They're using him the way they did before. But what the hell. I doubt Sandy minds being used. He didn't before and I doubt he minds now."

She looked at Celia. "Amazing, isn't it? How everything comes clear? It takes a while, but sooner or later it all comes clear. I threatened him. Did you know I threatened to leave him? You did? How? Doc, you did, too? Shit, I guess everybody knew everything. What Sandy was doing with his clients, everything."

Facing her made Doc's chest ache, made it hard to breathe. She said, "I threatened to leave and I would have, b-but he died first." Her mouth turned down, but suddenly it was up again. "Instead of threatening him, I should've hired him. Whew, heh heh. If I were a client, he'd have done anything for poor little me."

CHAPTER 30

A melia Drylie chose that moment to emerge from the graveside crowd. Millie took two steps toward her before coming back to tell Celia, "What a bunch of failures we are: when Sandy needed help I threatened him, you pretended he didn't exist and Doc…" She shrugged. "Doc was his usual self and offered him root beer." Then she stumbled toward Amelia Drylie.

"Jeez!" was all Doc could say.

Ellie asked Celia why her mother was staggering.

Celia put off the child's question. To Doc she said, "Millie's right, Jack. Admit it, she's right." She turned to deal with Ellie.

He watched Amelia and Millie as they approached each other, expecting a head-on collision.

But no. After slapping the dust from her hands, Amelia took Millie's hand, mumbled something to her, and sent a mock-kiss in Millie's direction that somehow missed by several inches.

Doc had never seen Amelia looking so relaxed, her face looking less hatchet-like. She nodded to Celia, ignored Doc as if he weren't standing there, and wandered off.

"Bitch!" Doc was thinking it but it was Millie who said it. "That damn woman, in fact all those damn women. Once they learned Sandy couldn't say no…"

Millie stepped away to endure condolences from other people.

Doc muttered to Celia, "Where's that bottle you took away from her? I need a drink."

It was Leo Drylie's turn. He began to rise on tiptoes to peck Millie's cheek and she bent to permit it. Drylie abruptly changed his mind and stuck out his hand; Millie gave it a single stiff jerk. She giggled as she watched him waddle away, but then her face sagged and her eyes grew moist and sad as a beagle's.

She asked, "Do you think…uh, did Sandy have to, you know, with his wife? With Amelia Drylie? Oh, my poor sweet Sandy."

Here it comes finally, Doc thought, the deluge of tears. Both he and Celia embraced her.

"There there now, that's okay, sweetie," Celia crooned. "Let it go, let it go."

"Better yet," Doc insisted, wanting to deprive those so-called mourners of the satisfaction of seeing the widow come unglued, "Let's get her outa here."

But it was not to be. Most of those who hadn't finished with Sanford Klein before were finally finished with him now; they had formed a line to say what Doc hoped would be a comforting word to the widow and child.

Doc glued his mouth into a smile at the first couple in line, County Solicitor Blumberg and the former Mrs. Blumberg, and kept it that way as one by one the people in line shook Millie's hand, pecked her cheek and, in the case of Ernie Norton, wheezed at her. Norton's approach frightened the child, who gratefully latched onto Doc's offered hand for protection.

Millie said, "It's so hard to figure people out. They can be so mean one minute, and the next..." A what-the-hell wave of the hand.

Doc couldn't help it, he couldn't let go completely. "I failed him, didn't I, Mil. I know I did. He was my good pal. My best friend. Why didn't he know he could count on me?" The answer he read in her eyes made him want to turn away.

The mourners returned to their cars. With Willie Hanrihan waving them through the entrance gate and Nuzzi's patrol car blocking highway traffic, they departed the cemetery. Leaving the Rabbi, Seamus and Willie, the Goldensons, Millie and Ellie Klein, and three laborers who were hanging idly around the backhoe as only men can hang around who were being paid time-and-a-half.

Seamus joined the Rabbi as he glumly trudged toward Millie. Both of their faces were drawn with fatigue. Seamus's voice was reedy thin.

He said, "This interment, Ma'am, well, I regret it from start to finish. 'Twas an insult, a blight on my reputation. Never, not once in my long career…"

Rabbi Kaye nodded gravely, as if he were adding gravity to the mortician's words; as if he too had a long career.

Seamus continued, "Well, I'll not soon live it down, sure'n I won't." He turned to depart.

Millie grabbed his sleeve. She said, "Please, Seamus, please don't feel that way. What happened wasn't any fault of yours, and I doubt you could have prevented it. Really." She stood very near him. Doc saw the daisy petals begin to flutter and her bosom press against Seamus's arm. "There's only so much a man can do. Believe me, I appreciate what both of you did." She pecked his cheek.

Doc had never before seen the mortician blush.

"If there's anything else, ma'am, anything at all…" Seamus asked.

Millie shook her head, and Seamus gathered up his son and headed for the now-empty hearse, leaving Rabbi Kaye behind.

Did Kaye expect a kiss too? Doc wondered if Kaye would stand there until he got one.

But no, he nodded at Millie and hurried after Seamus.

KLA KLA KLAK KLAK LARUM.

The backhoe clattered to life, startling Doc and the women; Little Ellie let out a yelp and grabbed onto Doc. A shiver shook Millie violently.

"Of all the ignorant…" Celia shook her fist at the backhoe operator. "Oh, what's the use. Let's go." She took Millie around the waist, took Ellie's hand, tried and failed to nudge Doc into motion. She pleaded with him, "What is it now?"

He said, "I can't just… just walk away and leave him. It's crazy, but… I can't." He shrugged his shoulders again and again, as if his coat collar were needling the nape of his neck. Doc thought to return to graveside, but he was startled to see the workmen begin to dismantle the tent.

KLA KLA KLA.

The backhoe clacked toward the grave with a claw full of clay and dirt. The appalling racket drove them all downhill to their car. Doc stopped at the driver's side door. Celia took his arm.

She said, "You're not going up there, Jack, and that's final. I don't see why you feel you can't leave him. Are you listening to me? I'm never sure you are." Doc kicked the left front tire.

Millie cozied up to him, too. She said, "Don't be so hard on yourself." She fluttered the daisy petals at him. "You were a really good friend, the only one he ever had." He shrugged. "It's true. Except for me, and wives don't count, you were the only friend he ever had. He loved you."

He kicked a pebble and watched it roll along the asphalt. "I loved him, too. I really did."

"Of course you did, and Sandy didn't need anything else from you. You didn't fail him. I'm sure Sandy never thought so."

Millie and Ellie—especially Ellie who seemed to prefer his hand to Celia's—were trying to make him feel better. He realized that and searched their faces for the lie—he saw none. He shrugged, smiled, and opened the car door for them. He said, "What say we get the heck outa here. My feet are killing me, and I'm thirsty, and I could eat something, too."

Millie said, "A little sherry would be nice right now." She looked wide-eyed at Celia as if for maternal permission.

Celia tried to be the stern disciplinarian, but she relented. "Well, maybe a little one." Millie clapped her hands. "But just one, you hear, Mil? A little one."

They drove out of the cemetery, leaving Sandy to the backhoe.

The End.

About the Author

Stephen was born, raised and educated in Pittsburgh, PA. After graduating from Pitt Dental School and serving a stint in the Army Reserve in the mid-60s, Stephen lived in, helped raise two children in and practiced family dentistry in Westmoreland County, which he jokingly calls Pizza County.

After nearly forty years there, Stephen and his wife, Shirley, finding themselves empty nesters, returned to the city of their first love, Pittsburgh, where they now reside.